F

curio:
WAR
It'll m

MW01048117

A surreal adventure like no other book you've read!
Rodney Appleseed views life through a silver eye.
Journey with him from nothingness straight into infinity!
Explore the breadth of heart, imagination and fun!
Then nestle into the point at which they intersect.

*"**I could NOT put it down!** It is the best book I have ever read. Thanks for putting a big smile in my heart :)"* -- Julie, RN

*"What a **unique** approach to life!!! I will pass your book on to my students. They each should have the opportunity to delve into such a **positive** story."* -- Linda, Teacher

*"**Creative**, insightful, **imaginative**, thought-provoking, innovative."* -- Choi, Semi-Retired

*"Moments of **genius**, actually."* -- Rocky, Graphics

*"Creative, a one of a kind... a **very special** ... approach to looking at the world around us."* -- Alice, Student

*"**Delightful** like a children's book, but not a children's book."* -- Marie

*"Philosophical, witty & spirited ... a very **innovative** writing style."* -- PingPing, HS Counselor

*"**Awesome!**"* -- Jennifer, Journalist

*"With so much cynicism & negativity around me all the time, it's nice to experience a character who's so **optimistic and hopeful**."* -- Tania, Coordinator

*"This book is definitely not linear. I've never read a book that somehow connects the tangents, distractions, and pure imagination we call thoughts. It really was very **enjoyable**."* -- Celeste, H.S. Math Teacher.

THE INFINITE ADVENTURES OF
RODNEY APPLESEED

in *NOTHING HAPPENS*

Congratulations
Bonnie
DREAM Big!
2003

by **Ross Anthony**

To The Magnificence of Life and The Spirit of Wonder

www.RossAnthony.com/books
For other Books, Essays & Articles by Ross Anthony

Special Thanks
Brian, Mrs. Pianza, "B," a Quaker guy, Marshall, HY Shaw, Philip

For other Arizona Blueberry books go to:
www.RossAnthony.com/books
ISBN 0-9727894-0-5
7/2003 (1stX,MMI)
10 9 8 7 6 5 4 3

CONTENTS

CHAPTER 1
LIKE A BULL IN A CANDY SHOP

Rodney could handle a bull. But only if the bull came from a place outside of his mind and occurred without warning, like potholes.

Gabe Jerson's Candy Shop Stop, where neighborhood kids could buy banana popsicles for forty-five cents and candy buttons at a quarter a foot off the roll, where Gunnison and Lemon sort of intersected: this was definitely not a place Rodney would expect to encounter any mammal larger than officer Baggio or Mrs. Devora carrying a couple bags of groceries.

Nonetheless, and without warning, the bull crashed out and into the street through the five by nine-foot picture window upon which Gabe had painstakingly hand-painted his name in brilliant red and green. The window shattered splendidly against the bull's nose, chips of broken glass jumped out into the grass and the gutter, already well littered with Tootsie Roll wrappers and bad Bazooka riddles. Cartons of Skittles and M&M's poured out onto the sidewalk.

Fortunately, none of this was happening in Rodney's mind -- that would have given him much too much time to think it over. No, Rodney was not thinking about bulls or Hershey's kisses or even banana pops; but he was, in fact, thinking, as always. Only moments prior to the bull's spectacular appearance, Rodney had been wondering about why people press the button in elevators when someone else has already pressed that button, " ... And it's even already lit up. So why press it again?"

Consequently, Rodney had just begun to think about how people never talk to each other in elevators and how even looking at another person there is an act of wasted awkwardness. (Rodney was pretty sure that awkwardness ought not be wasted.) " ... It's like a sideways glance is about the best anyone ever manages before they pretend to be relieving a crick in their neck or something. Their eyes just stay glued to the numbers above the door. How could we get people to talk to each other in an elevator? Is there something about elevators that make people unable to be friendly to one another? A force or an energy -- like pyramids or something?" Rodney wondered. (Rodney was very good at wondering.)

That's when the bull came into full view. Rodney instantly abandoned his train of elevator related thoughts, which he knew would be a shame, because runaway trains are quite difficult to regain control of (although it can be done). He knew that he was about to think some real good things in the elevator vein that he may never again be able to almost think -- even if he tried real hard to remember all the preliminary thoughts from around lunch time. But even for Rodney, very few brain impulses were needed for a value judgment between the immediate worth of elevator related thoughts and real live charging bulls with scratched noses: charging bulls seemed to warrant prompt attention.

"SAVE YOUR LIFE RODNEY!" blazing in red neon across trembling neurons, became the priority mental activity. Elevator contemplations scrambled for an open brain cell, but all brain cells were scrambling for an open path away from the bull. None were available. "Only -- maybe that fence, twenty yards to the left." Rodney knew he could easily climb that fence, but split-second estimates read negative for an attempt to reach it before the bull reached him. Another millisecond was lost considering Mrs. Denino's redleafed maple tree, but already the bull was between he and it. Rodney had to face this one on his own. Flushing from head to toe, he fought off a warming sensation from his crotch area, ripping off his red jacket, he grasped it firmly in both hands and waved the jacket in the air to his left.

Leaning his backside toward the beast, he felt its fur coat breeze narrowly by. To say that Rodney was terrified would be like calling the Grand Canyon a cranny. Rodney was clearly battling the urge to fall to the ground under the crushing weight of fear. Yet, he drew a certain confidence (and even satisfaction) in surviving the bull's first pass. The bull rounded and returned for the red, but this took some time -- enough for Rodney to almost reach the fence.

"One more 'OLE' and I'll be able to hop over!" Rodney surmised as he cocked his head at a jeering angle and proudly (even mockingly) dangled his red jacket. For that one small moment, he almost looked like a real matador. Had someone seen him there facing the bull head on, they certainly would have been impressed, even though his bony adolescent legs were knocking quite a bit at the knees.

The bull charged. Rodney leaned. One thousand pounds of crazed unpleasant-smelling animal snuggled against the small of Rodney's back and was gone. Rodney turned toward the fence and a brain cell freed.

"Which floor sir?" the fenceman asked.

"Over Please." Rodney replied.

"Over it is: Safety and Household Appliances."

Rodney quickly climbed the fence into an elevator full of people wearing red armor. "Why are you all wearing red armor?" he asked without for a second thinking that he should feel awkward.

"Well," the group answered (quite comfortable in their already old awkwardness), "There's a bull out there."

"Yes I know," Rodney was aware of that.

"So ... we need to protect ourselves," they responded a might bit on the defensive.

"But red attracts the bull and makes him angry," Rodney said dumbfounded.

"Yes, but if we remove the armor we will be naked against the bull," they argued.

"I see," Rodney began to understand their logic, "you could paint your armor another color."

"That would be a good idea. We didn't think of that," they nodded affirmingly and raised their eyebrows at each other.

Rodney continued the thought, "However, you would still be imprisoned in those metal garments."

Still nodding, "Yes, it does impede our movement a bit."

Confused with another thought, Rodney inquired as politely as he could, "Ahhhemm, by the way, why did you pick red?"

Several responses jumped about the elevator, but Rodney could only catch a few: "It was cheaper", "It goes well with my tie", and "It's my favorite color."

"Otherside: Safety and Household Appliances," the fenceman announced abruptly.

The elevator stopped. The fenceman politely pressed the DOOR OPEN button and Rodney stepped out, jamming the door with his foot as he turned to ask the now quiet group of red armor-wearing elevator passengers one last question, "So, ah, how long have you guys been goin' up and down in the elevator?"

"I've been here since the spring of 1979," one said.

"I came when my first marriage ended," said a second, "Sometimes my ex' brings little Bobby to visit me."

"I came on board straight out of college," said a third somewhat smugly.

"I see," said Rodney, "and what floor are you waiting to get out on?"

"Oh, we haven't thought about that -- there's a bull out there, you know."

"Yeah, I know," Rodney took his foot from the door. The doors closed and the OVER button was pressed, lit, and pressed three more times.

Rodney looked around. He had never been on this side of the fence before. He had thought of it once a couple of weeks before, but he was really hungry and late for dinner then. So this was a Rodney first. He loved firsts. Curiosity bursts out and runs amuck like lava during firsts. The food is always still warm and abundant during firsts. The excitement of innocence is at its height: ripe, red, ready to be harvested and eaten away never to be replaced with anything so white on the inside again.

Rodney walked over to a doghouse shaped like an old tugboat. "POPEYE" was carved above its door. He smiled in thought and spit out a few seeds, "Is it the nature of innocence to eventually be plucked away? Or should purity be savored and protected indefinitely? After all, there is such a beauty in innocence. A white light in a jungle of jagged darkness."

"On the other hand, it is quite difficult to live with -- innocence just isn't very smart. It hasn't any experience or background. Have you ever tried to strike up an intelligent conversation with innocence? It giggles and smiles and misses the point completely. Maybe there is a time when innocence needs to be filched? At that time can innocence do it alone? Does it need help from non-innocence? I don't think so -- the first innocence must have plucked itself away. How much fun would a world with only innocence be anyway?"

"And are there varying degrees of innocence? Or is it either innocent or not!? If there are levels, then where are the boundaries? And what happens if you change levels at the wrong time? Is there a wrong time? Are all times right? Or maybe only the time that happens ... no matter what time it is ... if it happens then it's right ... and maybe only if it doesn't happen at all is there a wrong time. Hmmm."

At that time, Rodney (in his normal juvenile form) was no longer in front of Popeye's tugboat doghouse. He had actually, physically, climbed into his own head. When the Johnsons found him two hours later, he had walked his feet all over the roof of his mouth until he'd swallowed most of his body from his toes to his rib cage. His hands had squeaked their way into his ears like Q-tips -- even past the elbows a little.

The Johnsons picked up the small ball that was Rodney and took him/it inside to look at more closely. They put it on the coffee table next to the stack of newspapers dated from Thursday the 8th of last year. Fortunately, they cleared the potato chips and Pepsi tabs from the area. They did not, however, remove the TV remote which held firm on channel 32: a "Murder, She Wrote" rerun.

"Should we call the police?" Eleanor Johnson asked.

Bill Johnson did not respond. He just sat there staring at Rodney, Bill's long bony legs bent, hands on his knees, neck out turtle-like, lower lip bending out and over like a diving board, studying the little ball of Rodney as if looking at it intensely enough would cause it to unravel.

"Should we call the fire department?" Eleanor asked.

Bill shook his head in stupor, "How do people do that to themselves?"

Eleanor tilted her head, "Maybe the loony house?"

"I think I got a crowbar in the shed," Bill Johnson leaned forward, all his weight on his big hands on his knees, straightening up, he ambled out the back door to the shed.

Eleanor mumbled, staring at the Rodney ball in disbelief. She reached out hesitantly toward it, but stopped just short of actually touching it. She paused, quickly withdrew her hand, folded her arms beneath her breasts and headed toward the kitchen still mumbling, "Maybe I should just make some soup ... "

"But what if there really is a wrong time? What if innocence were to be cut -- pried away when it shouldn't have been? Could there ever be a chance for a normal happy life again?" The ball that was Rodney began rolling about thrashing, spitting out apple seeds and picking up very fine potato chip crumbs in its hair.

"But! On the other hand, what if innocence never takes the plunge?! Never! Will the bearer be an infant all its life? A living walking embryo. Working and functioning, but never quite understanding the beauty of a mature full life ... Yin Yang and all that? ... Alive without knowing what it is to be alive?"

The Rodney ball rolled wildly back and forth. At the same exact time that Eleanor Johnson returned with a hot bowl of soup and Bill Johnson entered the room beating his palm with a crowbar, what was left of Rodney's left shoulder ran over the TV remote flipping the program to the cartoons channel, " ... yam and that's all that I yam ... "

"POPEYE!" Rodney's brain clicked, spontaneously warping him back to Popeye's tugboat doghouse.

Bill and Eleanor Johnson cleaned the seeds off the table and looked around the room for the Rodney ball. They gave it 4 or 5 minutes to return, before throwing their hands up and flipping the set back to 32. They sat back into chairs eroded to the shapes of their bone positions just in time for the exciting conclusion of "Murder, She Wrote."

"Shoot! We haven't seen that one in over a month," Bill was happy to realize.

"Hmmm." Eleanor said as she sipped her soup.

Rodney crawled into the doghouse.

The inside of this doghouse was surprisingly dim, damp and cool. Light didn't seep through the cracks in the walls as in most doghouses or treehouses. And this one was pretty big -- nearly large enough for Rodney to stand up straight. Not surprisingly, Rodney began to think to himself, "I can't see anything. It's dark and cold like ice. Like freezing water, I can feel my mind expand until it touches all the walls of the doghouse. When water becomes ice, the molecules line up in such a way that I could never understand. In such a way that it's bigger than it was at room temperature water, and therefore less dense, and therefore it floats. Which was an unfortunate thing for the people dining on the Titanic one evening. What if ice didn't float? What if it contracted like everything else that gets cold. Then it'd sink right to the bottom of your Coke ... and when you sipped with a straw you'd get cold Coke ... or if you decided to sip without a straw your lips wouldn't get overly cold. I think there must have been some mistake. Ice should sink. Excuse me God -- ice should sink! You messed up. I want this situation cleared up by Tuesday!"

Rodney grimaced oddly reflecting on a tangent,

"Probably I shouldn't joke like that -- I might end up in the dog house."

The doghouse slowed to a stop on Thomas Avenue. Rodney stepped out adjusting his lips. He walked over to the bus stop sign on the far corner in front of the new McDonald's, "279, 15, 310. Hmmm." Rodney knew that bus 280 went right to his front door, he pondered, "279 is almost 280. Could it be that 279 will get me almost home?" Rodney paused in that unlikely thought and a moment later bus 279 pulled up.

Just for fun, he boarded, tipped the driver and said with a smile, "My house, please."

The driver smiled too, beeped the horn twice, and while turning his head back to the street, pulled away, crushing a small party of red ants indulging over a water melon peel.

Rodney walked slowly towards the back of the bus winking an approving eye at a guy in blue and green plaid armor. The man winked knowingly back. To the right, a teenage couple embraced, kissing each other with jawbreakers in their mouths. Rodney reached over, tapped the girl on the shoulder, "Excuse me, may I have a jawbreaker, too?" The girl, a bit taken aback, slowly found another in the box and handed it to Rodney. He smiled, tilted his head and said, "Forgive me for the interruption -- please continue."

Behind the smooching teens, a man with a cane was arguing with himself concerning the choice of clothing he'd worn that day, saying that perhaps he really should have donned that yellow shirt his second wife had bought him the birthday before last. Although Rodney complimented him on his sharp look, the man did not seem to feel that the situation had been resolved.

Traffic became increasingly thicker until it no longer moved. The bus had been at a standstill for several minutes when Rodney noticed the "SLOW" sign at the side of the road. He looked up towards the driver and their eyes met in the mirror. Rodney pointed out at the sign and said facetiously, "Hey, slow down." The driver nodded, backed up a few feet and smiled at Rodney through the mirror. They both giggled a bit -- even though they were the only two who did.

With a sigh, Rodney leaned his head against the vibrating window. At first, the rhythm was relaxing, hypnotizing. He pretended to be a fourth-grader under forced hypnoses. His teacher had put him under in order to make him rat on the kid that shot the spit ball that struck the side of her neck when she turned her back to get the eraser. Mrs. Finkelstein had had enough of that kind of thing from the three classes prior and while whole classroom punishments were slightly satisfying she never singled out the runt who was shooting those spitballs.

"I, I was writing something ... something with a lot of capital letters ... oh, oh ... I was writing what you said, something like, .. don't pick your nose in class, something like, it's not terrible to pick your nose, but just don't do it in class. And then you turned to get the eraser, I think so that you could erase the long division problems from Friday so that you could start something new. 15,673 divided by 152, I think that was the last problem. So you turned, and I dropped the ink point out of my Bic. I had been sucking on that wad since Randy nailed me in the back of the head. But you turned and I loaded and I shot you. What a great shot. Right in the neck. Ha, I did it! Bet you thought it was Randy!"

The bus accelerated, the vibrations became annoying, leaving Rodney on the ever-so delicate edge of a headache.

"I knew it was you!" Mrs. Finkelstein squinted her eyes at Rodney as if to focus her disgust. (She really didn't know it was Rodney.) "I want to see you after school young man -- expect the worst!"

"You can't punish me. I'm still under hypnosis." Rodney stared blankly into space. Mrs. Finkelstein snapped her fingers and said, "Out of it ol' boy."

" ... And then you turned around, yes, yes, you turned around and pointed your finger at Randy ... " Rodney proceeded.

"Snap out of it Rodney!" The woman nervously demanded.

" ... And then you turned and pointed to me and now your punishing me with all the anger you have had for all those students that embarrassed you while your back was turned ... but you never caught them! I told you the truth and you direct all that anger at me and that's not fair. I can give you my recess, I can come after school, but I will not let you be that angry at me ... " Rodney spoke as if he'd swallowed honesty pills.

Mrs. Finkelstein frantically attempted to help poor Rodney to the drinking fountain in the hall.

" ... How could you let yourself be that angry at all? We're just kids. We don't think seriously about what we're doing. We don't hate you. You're just a teacher. Sometimes you take it all too seriously. Some day your anger will eat you up from the insides out -- like in the original 'Alien' ... "

Mrs. Finkelstein tried to get Rodney to drink, but his body was too limp. He just laid his head on the stainless steel refrigerated fountain. His head began rocking gently back and forth with the cycling of the freon and its ever-so relaxing hum.

"Wake up kid," a voice came from the front of the bus, "isn't that your house?"

Rodney's blurry blood-shot eyes met with the alert smiling eyes of the driver once again in the mirror.

"Oh! Oh! Thanks!" Rodney popped up.

The house was a rather common one, a bungalow with yellow brick and white gutters. The walk was marked with chalk, the lawn a bit long, but thick, with only a few yellow dandelions. An old woman sat in a rocking lawn chair on the small porch, knitting.

This street was not on the bus route -- everyone on the bus knew that except Rodney (he had never taken the 279). But then, Rodney was the only one who knew that the house was not his.

The bus driver smiled as Rodney jumped out, ran up the porch and hugged the old woman. And then nothing happened.

Nothing happened.

The bus had gone, the grass had grown just a little bit longer and Rodney sat himself on the steps of the porch.

"You are not my son, you know..." remarked the woman.

"I know ma'am, because you are not my mom." Rodney replied. "Do you have a son?"

"Yes, as a matter of fact, I do have a son." she smiled.

"Tell me about him." Rodney pulled his knees up and wrapped his arms around his shins. "What's his name?"

"Benj ... Benjamin. He's twenty-seven. He's in Thailand or Taiwan or something like that -- teaching English and playing flute in the subways."

"When's he comin' back -- do you know?" Rodney asked.

"Maybe next year. Hmmm. Well, he's having fun and that's real important. How many people do what they really like?"

"I sure don't know," Rodney answered, "Would you like some apple seeds so that you could mail one to him? He could plant it, and then every time he watered it, he could think of you."

The woman left her thoughts and looked Rodney square in the eyes, "Why yes, young man, I'd really like that."

"And you could plant one here in your front yard so that every time you water it you could think of him."

She laughed, "I don't need a tree to think of Benj."

"But when he comes back to the States and sees the tree ... well, he'll just feel really loved." Rodney proposed.

The woman smiled approvingly at Rodney, " ... And your mother, tell me about her."

"My mom? My mom? Let me tell you about my mom. My mom's awesome. She's fifty and she still plays racquetball and no one in our family can beat her. She does Cub Scout stuff for us even when she wants to maybe do something else. She's always concerned about me. Even, sometimes, I think it's too much. But mostly she knows when to trust me. I guess a lot of kids aren't so lucky -- 'cause they got moms that do some strange stuff."

The woman nodded.

Rodney popped up, "Hey you wanna play hopscotch?"

"Sure would!" The woman replied.

"1,3,4&5,6,7&8,9 Sky Blue!" The afternoon surrendered to dusk and a salmon peach swam across the horizon.

"1,4&5,6,7&8,9 Sky Blue!"

Rodney reached in his pocket and picked out a

packet of apple seeds. He held it by the string and lowered it into the old woman's palm, " ... And if I ever take bus 279, I'll be able to find you again ... if you plant the tree, you know."

The woman held the seeds in her warm hands, "I'll keep the chalk here on the sidewalk."

The peach salmon swam away into the sky blue night.

CHAPTER 2
DRIVING TO INFINITY

Rodney walked to the nearest pay phone and called his mom, "Hi mom. I'm a bit lost. Can you come get me?"

She yelled a little, but he didn't mind that much -- he knew that she was just worried. Rodney read the street names off the corner post, while his mother took a few breaths to calm down, "Rodney! Okay Rodney, stay right where you are. I'll be there in about ten minutes. Be careful. I heard on the news that a wild bull had escaped and is running loose in the neighborhood."

Rodney leaned against the door to the telephone box, "Phones are so crazed. I could speak to just about anyone on the planet if I wanted to. Life must have been really different before phones."

Reaching into his pocket for another coin, Rodney

dialed his friend Randy.

The phone rang twice. The answering machine clicked on, "Hello, this is the Olsen's residence. We're not in right now, please leave a message after the beep, which might take a while, this is an old machine ... BEEP."

"Hi, this is Rodney for Randy," Rodney began. "Well, it's not actually Rodney. What you are now listening to is magnetic particles on tape that are arranged in such a way that they sound just like my voice when connected to analog electronics. Isn't that crazed!? You are hearing a pretty good representation of my voice now, which is a different now than the now I am now using to record on your tape. In my now, I'm here in a telephone box lost, but in your now, I'm probably home having dinner. Isn't that crazed?"

Rodney hung up, held up his last coin, and studied it in the light of dusk that passed through the scratched windows of the old style telephone box. There was an itch in his arm as he held the coin over his head. He imagined that an eagle had landed there and perched on his shoulder.

Rodney put the coin back into his pocket. Staring blankly at the graffiti on the wall just behind the phone, he noticed a single phone number without a name or a message so just for fun he called it.

A voice greeted him, "Hello, this is God, can I help you?"

"I'm not sure." Rodney responded.

"Well then, why did you call?"

"I just saw this phone number here on the wall, so what the heck? I tried it."

"So ... it's my number, you sure you don't want anything?"

"Well, I mean, why would your number be here? I mean if you really are God and not some weirdo. Anyone can leave a number here and answer the phone any way they feel like it. Geeze, you shouldn't even need a phone."

"Is that how you're gonna be then? I'm asking you nicely if you want anything and you're calling me a weirdo?"

"I wasn't calling you a weirdo. I'm just saying how do I know that you aren't some weirdo?"

"You could have had anything, kid. I asked what you wanted. You could have had all the answers to every question in the universe if you wanted, but instead, you just go and fill the universe up with more questions. I really don't like to be doubted. It gets on my nerves. It's almost worse than being taken for granted." Irked, the voice paused. "Anyway, I love you. What else can I do? It's my job."

"I'm sorry about the doubting thing, but some kind of proof shouldn't be too much to ask. Shouldn't it?" Rodney queried feeling a bit tacky.

"I forgive you," came the reply in unison with a crashing sound that the shattering glass created. Rodney covered his head with his forearms as every window in the telephone booth burst into a million splattering pieces. Some of the crystal chips ascended so high that they appeared to be swallowed by the limitless blue sky. The rest of the splinters fell all around the box, simulating the sound of drum cymbals. For a split second a hot white star shot through the sky. Rodney opened his eyes just in time to see a tall thin girl with long black hair step away giggling. He couldn't see her face, but he did notice the small slingshot in her back pocket. He took a deep sigh, collapsed to a crouching position and picked up a single stone that was still rocking on the floor of the booth.

He held the stone up to his eyes, "I s'pose that could have been an amazing coincidence. Either that, or I shouldn't have been so demanding," Rodney thought as he slid the stone into his pocket, "but I guess I just needed to be sure. I mean, God -- that's pretty serious." Rodney picked up the dangling receiver only to hear the disconnect tone, "Shoot! I forgot to ask about the ice cube thing!"

"Rodney? Rodney?"

Rodney rolled his head toward the slowing car, his mom leaned over the seat to look out the passenger side window.

"Come on Rodney, get in."

Rodney slid into the big car gritting a bit in shame.

"My goodness, Rodney, how did you get all the way over here? Now get in and put your seat belt on."

Rodney made a strange face and turned his eyes toward his feet.

"Really Rodney, what if you didn't have any money to call me -- you got me worrying, young man."

Images of trees glazed across the top of the windshield as Rodney tried to make the streetlights run into marks on the glass by positioning his head in different ways.

The big car entered the highway. Rodney's mom began thinking of what she'd make for dinner and how she'd still be able to pick up Rodney's little sister from music practice and get those papers to Mr. Albers at Jefferson Park.

"DON'T DRIVE INTO SMOKE," a highway sign warned.

"Mom, why aren't you s'posed to drive into smoke?"

"Well, why do you think?"

"Maybe the smoke is poisonous, and you'll die?" Rodney toyed. "Or maybe the smoke will stain the upholstery? Or choke the engine? Or disintegrate the tires?"

"I suppose that those are possible," Rodney's mom began, "but, I was told that you don't drive into smoke because maybe there is a wrecked car inside it that you can't see or maybe the road turns -- so it's really dangerous to drive into smoke."

She looked toward Rodney to see if he was satisfied with that answer, but instead she found him fast asleep.

"DON'T DRIVE INTO SMOKE." In Rodney's

dream he was driving on the highway with his mom, which might seem like a waste of a good dream, because it exactly duplicated reality. He could have woken up and not even have known it. Actually, he had fallen asleep and didn't even know it.

"DON'T DRIVE INTO JELLYFISH," cautioned another sign.

"Jellyfish? Mom do Jellyfish drive?"

"I don't think so, but anyway it's probably a good idea not to drive into 'em."

Yet another sign alerted, "DON'T DRIVE INTO INFINITY."

"Infinity? Mom, you know what infinity is?"

"Well, they explained it to me when I was a little girl, but I didn't quite understand it. Keep watching the signs. Maybe we'll get a chance to find out."

Rodney knew what infinity was, but thought that actually seeing it might be fun so he shut his mouth and leaned forward, putting his face against the windshield so that his lips and nose scrunched up.

"1ST AVENUE 2 MILES"

"1ST AVENUE THIS EXIT"

"INFINITY NEXT 3 EXITS"

"Mom!"

"Yep! I see it." Rodney's mom answered and she exited the highway into infinity.

As the '89 Volvo wagon, drove off exit ramp "N-2" toward Southern Infinity, the colors on the trees and grass and everything began to drain into black and white. Red, blue, green, beige, they all dripped out of the leaves, and from Rodney's hair and skin, and the glove compartment until everything, even Rodney and his mom, were just black and white.

"Wow! I never imagined infinity would be in black and white." Rodney's mom said with surprise and a gray smile.

The colors formed puddles on the street and then evaporated into the sky.

"WELCOME TO INFINITY"

"TOLL 500 FEET"

"TRUCKS KEEP RIGHT"

Rodney's mom pulled into the nearest booth. A man in a gray uniform and a flashlight lazily searched the car, "Any Color ma'am?"

"No sir, just us."

"Good then, that'll be five apple seeds," the man requested.

Rodney reached into his pocket and gave the man seven. The man smiled at Rodney like the bus driver and said, "You are truly a gentleman sir -- may I have your name?"

"Then what will I use?" Rodney joked, "... just kidding. I'm Rodney."

"And I'm Rodney's mom," Rodney's mom added grinningly.

"My pleasure indeed, I am Hogan --- Hogan NSpace," the man introduced himself proudly. "So ... what brings you folks to infinity?"

"Oh, we just thought we'd drop by on a whim." Rodney's mom answered.

"This doesn't make any sense!" Rodney burst. "Infinity ain't a place -- it's a concept! And it's infinity's very nature that you could never reach it -- especially never in a Volvo!"

"There's actually another way to get here, but the way you've done it is easier and quicker even if you stay under the speed limit." Hogan replied.

"I can't believe it. How can you get to infinity in a car? Scientists haven't even figured a feasible way of getting out of the solar system!"

"If you trust that this is not, in fact, infinity, then you are implying that I'm not real -- that I don't even exist. Well then, let me tell you, I'm offended. I'm insulted. What nerve you have -- calling me a liar."

"I didn't call you a liar."

"You did indeed! You don't trust that I am. You doubt me. That is very sad for both of us. I do exist and I'm worthy of your respect. Just as you exist. You must also question yourself then ... with whom are you conversing, if in your logic I must not be?"

"This is confusing me! Hogan, I'm really trying, but I can't make sense of it."

"Well, that's better -- at least it's honest. You did call me by name -- I guess I feel better. Let me tell you Rodney, because I like you, because you have something special between your ears that shimmers a bit out your eyes, what will it hurt you to let me be real?

Even if I were not, as your logic wants you to believe -- what would it hurt to let me be real?"

"Hogan, I truly don't get it! And yet, I like you too -- I think."

"Then let me be real, Rodney. It's such a small thing. And it'll be to the benefit of both of us. I really shouldn't have to ask at all -- do the squirrels ask your permission to scurry up the trees? And then just because they are on the opposite side of the trunk where you can't see 'em -- does that mean they don't exist as well? Rodney, let me be real."

"Mr. NSpace, you seem very nice. I mean, I like you. Forgive me for offending you -- believe me, I wasn't trying to do that at all! I can't easily forget what I learned. It's not easy for me to understand your existence; but, I want to try. I really will try."

Hogan NSpace leaned back with a sigh and change of expression. "Well, that ain't a supernova, but I suppose it'll do. Anyway, It's my job to tell you to leave at dusk. This is for your own safety."

"Do bad things happen at night here?" Mrs. Appleseed queried.

"No not really. Well, what I mean is ... when it gets dark in infinity -- it gets real dark. So dark that you can only see nothing. Actually, it is exactly correct to say that when infinity gets dark -- it becomes nothing." Hogan paused and looked Rodney straight in the eyes, "And if you thought infinity was hard to comprehend -- you better keep yourself out of nothing for a while."

"Are you gonna stay in nothing?" Rodney asked.

"Sure will. I have for many years. It takes a lot of preparation. You can't go into nothing with a mind full of expectations. Unfortunately, many folks do just that."

"What happens to 'em." Rodney wondered out loud.

"They go completely insane. They scramble pathetically for something before it's time for something. Mostly always they end up finding anything, only to discover it's not something they wanted at all."

"So how can you do it? How can you get into nothing and come back out okay, like you are now?"

"You just can't cast any expectations out into nothing. It's okay to have a few -- but they must be carefully chosen. If you choose them unwisely -- you'll find out the first night in nothing. Instead, fill yourself with patience and trust. Patience, because eventually, at dawn, nothing becomes everything, and without fail, everything becomes infinity."

"Whoa heavy stuff, Hogan."

"Yea, I know ... and trust, because out there in the middle of nothing -- it's not so hard to start believing that nothing will always be nothing and that nothing will eventually become of it. Rodney, you must always believe in the dawn, otherwise you will scramble for anything."

"Hogan, don't worry about it -- we ain't going in there -- remember?"

"All right then, the other thing that my job requires me to tell you is that as you leave infinity you must drive into a rain cloud."

"Why's that?"

"When you came here your color drained from you and formed puddles on the road. Those puddles evaporate throughout the day -- and make rain clouds."

As the two gentlemen spoke, Rodney's mother gently dozed off.

"So the rain will restore our color?"

"You got it Rodney. The only two things that have color in infinity are the clouds and the sun. But only the clouds can restore your color. Now don't forget to leave before dark and you might want to let your mom sleep a while longer; she looks a bit over worked."

"Yea, she is. She works really hard all day and then me and my sister don't even thank her. It's like we think it's just her job to cook for us and clean our clothes and stuff. We love her, Hogan, we really do, but I wish we'd show her a little more appreciation."

"Well Rodney, sounds like you're further on your way to doing just that than most kids. Not all moms care enough to do all that good stuff, you know," Hogan tilted his head making sure Rodney could get a good deep glimpse of his narrowed eyes, "My mother never lifted ... actually she wasn't even ever ..." Hogan paused, his eyes relaxed and a smile broke out on his face. "Rodney, you look tired as well. You learned a lot today, why don't you take a nap too. I'll wake you at dusk. Thanks for letting me be real."

CHAPTER 3
NOTHIN' BUT DIRT

Rodney's heavy eyelids slowly lowered. The sun became a melting glob of yellow wax as it struggled to keep its head above the horizon. Some of the wax became liquid and ran into the troughs of a corrugated field of dirt. A farmer sat, head in hands, on a fifty-one year old John Deere tractor that hadn't moved in two years.

"Hey, what's up?" Rodney popped in an attempt to breathe some spirit into this dismal scene.

"Nothin's up boy, nothin' but dirt." The farmer mumbled as he snared at the impotent yellow wax.

"I'm sorry sir, I don't understand."

"Yea, well, you're still a youngen."

"Nonetheless sir, I still enjoy understanding."

The farmer turned to get a better look at Rodney. "You enjoy understandin' -- do ya boy?"

"Yes sir, I do."

" ... Crit'cal thinkin', enligh'enment and all the like?"

"Yea, I think so. Well actually I think a lot -- sometimes I even get yelled at because of it."

"Yea, maybe you can help me understan'."

"Sir?"

"I'm fifty-one. 'Been around as long as this here tractor. She use'ta be a beaut', full o' spirit, full o' spunk. Look at her now -- rusty, worn, motionless in mud. I use'ta be full o' spirit too. I use'ta love this land -- get down on my knees, run my hands through this dirt like it was the hair on the heads o' mah chil'en. This land use'ta give acres o' food, acres o' pride, acres o' securi'y for me and mah family. Sometimes at the end of a day like this one here, I would jus' take a run through these fields with my hands a wavin' in the air and thankin' God for his plentiful luv and mah spirited strength. Heck, you know, when no one was lookin', I'd roll in the mud with the pigs jus' 'cause I was so excited about this here good field, this here good life."

"And now sir?"

"Now mah tractor hasn't moved in pert-near two years. Now this here field has produced nothin' but dirt for two years. Now I's jus' an old man, with pain in mah back. The spirit in mah heart done given itself up to the dusk -- to the night. I's tired son, I's real tired. These here past two years, I been plantin' seeds in this field. Even when most folks was tellin' me to go inta dairy. I can't go inta dairy boy, I luv this land. I been plantin' seeds, but nothin' growed. Nothin's 'come o' mah hopes. I's completely frustra'ed, disappoin'ed and jus' plain 'xhaus'ed. I took the risk o' stickin' with this stubborn field. I really believed that if I jus' kep' plantin' those seeds -- all kinds: corn, wheat, cabbage, peas, everythin', anythin' -- that 'ventually one o' 'em would grow. I done believed that true."

"Don't you believe that anymore?"

"Son, I's tired. I sown mah life, mah spirit, mah passion away. After while o' seein' nothin' come o' your work -- you tend to lose belief."

"And understanding?"

"Seems like once belief goes, understandin' gets up and takes a hike as well."

"And then hope?"

"And then, God forgive me, luv o' life and self."

"So that the only thing left is despair and insanity."

The farmer, squinting one eye, grunted sarcastically, "Geeze boy, you's a real pick-me-up, let me tell ya."

"Sir, I can't make your field turn. But, I do know a bit about planting seeds. And maybe it's only because I'm young, but I love planting seeds even if they bounce off the ground, even if there is no sign of their taking root. Because I haven't forgotten the joy simply in the planting -- have you?"

"'Surely have forgotten. But ya know, 'feels good to be reminded -- thank ya."

"And I recently learned something that I did not completely understand -- but perhaps you will."

"Well let's give it a listen, son, I ain't got nothin' but time."

"Nothin'? Nothin' eventually becomes everything and everything eventually becomes infinity. And that has to do with patience and trust and something about how wisely you select your expectations. Does that make any sense to you sir?"

"Hmm, sure's a mouthful for a boy your age -- shoot, even for a grown man. Surely boy, I understan'. I understan' 'xactly. And I'd take a bet you will too -- but right now you's really jus' too young to 'preciate that there mouthful."

"Uh sir, there's one more thing that I'd like to do with your permission."

"Surely boy, what's it?"

"I'm partial to apple seeds. Would you allow me the pleasure of planting a few in your field?"

The farmer paused, looked Rodney straight in the eye while the dry parched ridges of his own moistened, "Son, I'd be honored."

Rodney turned to the field with a hop in his step. He pulled his full fist from his pocket and began to plant each seed delicately and carefully. The dusk had already pressed the yellow wax glob against the horizon so that it became long and thin like a crayon. Rodney then began to run and spin, letting the seeds jump out between the cracks in his fingers. When all the seeds had left his grasp, Rodney waved his hands through the gray air, over the black field. The crayon colored the tips of his fingers yellow, as well as the top of the tractor's steering wheel and the strands of the farmer's hair that wafted gently in the air. The yellow became orange and then red and then the crayon left the sky in exchange for a fist full of stars.

The sky shimmered in the starlight and dimming sunlight like a plate of glass. Rodney watched as a huge hand came from above the massive sheet of glass and tapped on it twice. "Rodney, it's dusk."

Rodney rolled down the window, "Hogan! Hogan!"

"Rodney," Hogan continued, "it's dusk, wake up your mother. It's time for you to go."

"Hogan!" Rodney choked on too many thoughts at once.

"Don't worry Rodney, It's been a pleasure meeting you." Hogan winked, his eye twinkling like a star.

"Mom! Mom! We gotta go!"

Mrs. Appleseed awoke startled. She started the car while Rodney looked back, but Hogan was gone.

At that moment, a relatively small rain cloud dislodged from the sky and floated right down to the highway. Rodney's mom drove directly into it. Immediately, moisture collected on the windows, Rodney could even taste the rain.

"Red Rodney!" Rodney's mom exclaimed, "it tastes like red,"

Rodney laughed with one blue eye, "Ha, only your mouth is red, mom, the rest of your color hasn't come back yet -- you look real funny!"

"Me? You should see yourself with only one blue eye!"

"SLOW" warned the sign, but the two were laughing and watching each other changing hue -- they didn't see the sign. The rain cloud dissipated and the Volvo came to a stop at the next toll.

"Yes, pleasant young man, is it apple seeds you'd like?" Rodney's mom, now quite giddy, asked playfully to the man at the booth.

"No, thanks ma'am, just your hand." replied the pleasant young man with a grin.

"Well, I'm flattered, but I'm sorry, I'm married. This is my son."

"I'm married too ma'am. I have two sons, a daughter and a tank full of fish. It's my job to stamp your hand so that you can come back to infinity without the nominal five seed cover charge."

"Oh, I see." Rodney's mom said, glancing shortly at Rodney who had laughed so hard he had sprayed the inside of the windshield with his saliva and little bits of chewed apple seeds. She extended her hand out the window as if she were tipsy from wine -- as if she expected it to be kissed. The pleasant young man routinely stamped it.

"You should have slowed a bit before that cloud dissipated." the man stated.

"Why's that?" said Rodney's mom.

"It would have given the color a bit more time to fill in your son's left eye."

Rodney adjusted the rearview mirror. He looked into his own eye to see only gray -- with bits of silver shavings.

"Silver's quick, you know -- quick silver, but blue is so moody. Blue will drag its feet all day in self-pity. And still sometimes it jumps. It just jumps. Looks like you got both sides of blue in your eyes son," the pleasant young man paused. "We hope you've enjoyed your day in infinity -- you all come back now. Remember our two locations: just past the last molecule in the universe and just an inch or two south of the top of your head, juxtaposed askew between your ears. Ciao bambinos."

CHAPTER 4
TOROS!

The Volvo once again entered the familiar highway. All the colors of the road began to look the same as they always had since Rodney could remember. All the signs began to make fine legal sense without trying to convey any philosophical statements.

Rubbing his eyes, Rodney wrestled with the idea that he hadn't actually slept and that he just might have been the first kid on his block to have reached infinity. Rodney's mom pulled off the highway to a familiar cobblestone street not far from home and stopped at the red light.

"Hmmm. A red light." Rodney reflected, "What is it with red? It makes bulls charge, but stops people. Is that the nature of red? I think I tasted red once. I don't think red stops people. I don't stop when I see a red car, or a redwood, or a redhead. I think people stop because they all agreed to stop at little red lights on street lamps. Because, before red lights there probably were many problems at intersections. So some people probably sat down and said we need to all agree to stop at some color. 'How about blue?' someone might have said. 'Why not?' Perhaps some people argued strongly for blue -- but apparently red won out. And the blue supporters now must stop at the red anyway. How humiliating. Or maybe not, maybe they realize that the organization is more important than the detail of color. After all, red works just fine."

Rodney turned to his mother, "Mom, do you think that if in the future cars have anti-accident devices installed so that they can change levels at intersections or warp through them -- do you think that it will be okay not to stop at a red light?"

"Well Rodney, it's the law to stop at a red, and it's just common sense too."

"But, what I mean is, what if things changed so that it was pointless to stop at an intersection. Like technology had fixed things so that there were no more accidents and cars could just pass through each other like ghosts go through walls or something like that. Should you feel guilty if you don't stop at a red light, if maybe everyone just forgot to take the traffic lights down?"

"Rodney, you've got a point there." Rodney's mom paused in thought. "Actually, that reminds me of the way I used to make pot roast on Tuesdays. Remember the Tuesday night pot roast?"

"Yea, but I don't exactly see how that relates to red."

"Every time I cooked pot roast, I'd season it just like my mom did. I'd add wine just like my mom did, and I'd cut the ends off of each side just like my mom did."

"Yea, so is it so unusual to learn to cook from Gramma?"

"I did that for years, fifty-two Tuesdays a year, I'd cut the ends off the pot roast and I didn't quite know why. Until one Tuesday, your Gramma cooked with me. We seasoned the pot roast, we soaked it in wine and then I began to cut the ends off."

"Yea, so?"

"So, Gramma stops me and says, 'Why are you cutting the ends off?' And I say, 'Because you always cut the ends off when you made pot roast.' Then your Gramma started to laugh strongly and she finally says, 'I cut the ends off because the roast was always too big to fit in my little pans.'"

"Ha, so even though you had big enough pans you still cut the ends off -- just by rote, just by tradition, just by rule."

"Yep. So maybe you're right Rodney. Rules should be rethought from time to time to see if they still apply. And I think that in your future idea, you shouldn't feel guilty if you don't stop at a red."

The light turned green and a crowd of Spanish men dressed in white with red bandannas ran past the Volvo on both sides and even a few men ran across the top of the car.

Rodney cracked his window and shouted, "What's going on?"

"Toros! Toros!" the Spanish men cried, laughing and screaming.

"What's 'Toros' mom?"

Rodney's mom stayed stopped at the green light as the flow of Spanish men in white continued, "I think it's Spanish for 'bulls'."

"Bulls?"

The pace of the flow of Spanish men increased as did the size of their eyes and their frantic dodging motions until Rodney could see at the rear ends of the last few runners a group of charging bulls gushing over the cobblestone like lava.

Rodney waited till the rambling crowd of men and bulls had passed out of sight around the corner and then rolled down his window. One last runner who had been bumped by the bulls slowly pulled himself up from the street rubbing his elbows and limping.

"What's going on?" Rodney asked him.

"Que? No Comprendo." The man replied.

"What is going on here?" Rodney repeated.

"He doesn't understand you," a tall Native American girl sitting on the fence shouted. "He speaks only Spanish."

"Spanish?"

"Yes, he is from Pamplona in Spain. It is his tradition to run from the bulls in the streets once each year." She continued as she walked to Rodney's window and leaned against the car. "Oh, you have beautiful eyes -- one is almost only silver."

"Really?" Rodney shrugged a little in embarrassment, but was too curious to become completely shy. Anyway, he had already decided a couple of months ago that being shy wasn't such a good strategy for learning things, and that if he had a question in his head --then he should ask it. "I don't get it, why would people do somethin' so dangerous on purpose -- isn't that kind of stupid?"

"Traditions can be very powerful things," Rodney's mom added, "and while it is true that some traditions have lost their original purpose, there still are many traditions that have a lot of good meaning for people."

Rodney scrunched his eyes, "Yea ... but running in front of bulls! That's dangerous -- I know! These people could be killed!"

"Yes, it is possible, but not likely," the girl explained, "Mostly, just bruised," her tone turning stern, "You should be careful not to condemn things just because you don't understand them, or disagree with them or think that they are stupid. There are so many different cultures and languages on this planet -- if you close your mind to them you will miss out on a greater understanding of yourself. Do not think your culture is the most important one."

"What are you talking about?"

"Every country that makes a map of the world

places its own nation in the center. But, in fact, the globe is round and spins and has no center. All nations share it and are of equal importance. Just because you speak English and play baseball, do not think badly of people who do not. And don't think that dodging bulls in the street is stupid. Don't you remember the feeling you had when the bull brushed passed the small of your back earlier today, Rodney?"

"How did you know about that?"

"What? Did you think I am real? You silly adolescent. Did you think that it was normal to have Pamplonans running through your city? I am a dream. You are sleeping. You are so beautiful with one eye of silver. I will call you 'Shining Eye'."

And the Indian girl bowed her head into the car and kissed Rodney's forehead.

"I feel stupid now. I really do. It's just a dream. I have a problem that way. I have a hard time distinguishing my dreams from life."

"Then don't. Let it all be important."

"That would be nice. Because, then you would be more like real. And then I could maybe see you again. Because, I feel some kind of warmth from your face, from your skin."

"My *red* skin."

"Yea, isn't that funny, your red skin."

"Then see me again if you like, but now I must go, you are about to wake up. Your mother will tap you on the shoulder soon."

"What is your name?"

"Guess ... And you will be right."

"Warm Face."

"Right."

"Rodney? Rodney? Your ears are red. Are you all right? We're home honey. Come on get up."

"Hi mom, I love you."

"I love you too, Rodney. Now, come on, I've got to get dinner together and pick up your sister and something else I can't remember. Hey, isn't that your friend Randy?"

"Yep."

"Why don't you play with him and then come in for dinner in about half an hour."

"Sure, mom. -- Hey, Randy!" Rodney shouted as he stepped out of the '89 Volvo that had just been through infinity.

"What's up Rodster?" Randy called back over his shoulder while fiddling with the water hose.

"Man! did ya see the bull that crashed through Jerson's store?" Rodney blurted as he stepped up to Randy.

"No, but I heard about it. They still ain't caught 'im. They got police on it and everything." Randy updated. "Speaking of police, I got an idea."

"Randy, Randy, Insanity Randy, What's it this time?"

"Well Rodster, the cops keep circling the block," Randy started, "it's making me paranoid," he paused to make sure the water from the hose was going into that little hole on the back of his translucent green squirt gun, "soooo ... "

"So you want to ambush the cops!!??"

"Crazed, huh? What'da ya say? Grab the orange one -- it's full already," Randy spouted as his eyes ignited with dare.

"I got no problem with the cops. Why should I attack them with water pistols?"

"You didn't have no problem with Old Finkelstein back in fourth grade -- that was a great shot, man!"

"Yep, it was an unforgettable shot -- but we were idiots then. I'm not a fourth grader anymore."

"Rodster? Hot Rod? Where's that zest for life? You used to be so bold!"

"I still am bold. You just can't see me bold. You just see the same old Rodney here before you with messy blonde hair and torn jeans with a thinking look on his face. If you really wanted to have fun ... you'd crawl inside my head."

"Whoa Rodster, don't go off getting all psycho on me. I don't want ya to make my brain hurt again -- I just wanna drench some cops."

"You know you're just having fun, but will they? They fight real live bad guys all the time. They're always worrying that maybe they're gonna get shot. They're more paranoid than even you. When you're in trouble you call them, but when they're in trouble -- who are they gonna call?"

"Hot Rod, it's water!"

"If you swing at a bee, don't cry if you get stung."

"You're no fun anymore, man! I don't know if I wanna hang around with you anymore."

"I'm fun, Randy. You just want me to be fun right now with this particular idea. And if you really feel like you don't want to be my friend because I won't squirt the cops -- then take off -- I don't need that kind of friend."

"Awe come on Roddy, what if the officers don't mind -- what if they really would like it? Think it's fun? Cool off a bit?"

"Then I'd do it."

"So how are we s'posed to know if they'd like it."

"Ask."

"Yea right," Randy joked, "hey coppers, mind if we squirt you guys?"

"Randy, you'd be surprised how much people miss out on simply because they don't bother to ask. I'm not guaranteein' anything, but so what if they say 'no'? There'll be another squad car around in a bit anyway."

"Okay then, Mr. Cerebral -- you ask!"

With instinctual timing, a patrol car slowed to the two boys. One of the officers lowered his window, "Hey you two, have you seen a bull around here?"

"Not lately officer," Rodney replied politely, "uh, by the way, would you guys mind if we ambushed you with our squirt guns?"

"You mean we drive around the block and you

unload your water pistols through our windows?"

"Yea, all in fun ... " Randy added.

"All in fun ... " the officer reiterated, nodded and smiled.

Randy's eyebrows darted upward in amazement, "Crazed! I can not believe this!"

While the Squad car pulled away around the corner, the second officer rolled his window up and said something that was kind of difficult for the two boys to hear.

"Did he say, 'We'll be right back'?" Randy asked.

"Actually, I thought he said, 'As long as we get to shoot back,'" Rodney cautioned.

"No, No, they couldn'ta said that. We're just stupid teenagers, and besides, we asked nicely. Probably they said something like, 'Prepare for your attack.'" Randy reasoned. "Anyway, we asked and they looked like they didn't mind, so you gotta attack Rodney, you said you would."

"I said I would, so I will."

The two soft-skinned young people pulled a large broken tree trunk out into the street. Randy hid under the stairs to his front porch and adjusted the nozzle on his hose. Rodney rolled a dumpster out to the curb, hid inside and licked the water on the outside of that little fill hole on the back of his squirt gun.

Blue and white squad 916 rounded the corner slowly, "PFSHT, Squad 916 approaching obstruction in roadway at 4800 block of Lemon Avenue," Officer

Hanes radioed in just for fun.

"Proceed with caution, Hanes, that's the approximate location Insanity Randy was last seen, over, PFSHT," the radio responded.

"PFSHT, Insanity Randy? The notorious spitball and all-liquids hitman?" Hanes inquired.

"The very same. He's hosed and dangerous, men. If your mommies told you not to get wet today, we advise you to leave the area immediately, out, PFSHT," headquarters finished.

"Well Baggio, I say we take this kid."

Baggio turned his head to Hanes, nodded with a stiff chin and pulled his 44 police revolver from its holster.

Squad 916 stopped at the tree trunk in the road. The officers rolled their windows down to get a better look.

"BONSAI!" Randy cried as a stream of cold clear water shot through the passenger side window wiping officer Baggio's cap right off his head. Rodney peeked over the top of the dumpster squirting spurt after spurt into officer Hane's eyes until his squirt finger started to hurt.

The officers ducked inside the car and waited for Rodney's pistol to empty. And then, just as Randy made his move for better position, Hanes and Baggio emerged from their squad, wielding their revolvers.

They spotted Randy first, firing three rounds each as the boy dove into a concrete stairwell. Another three rounds each went into the staircase just above him. By that time, Rodney had nearly warped to safety behind his house's brick fence.

"Geeze, they really shot back!" Rodney said quietly to himself as the officers returned their warm guns to their holsters, removed the tree from the road, tipped their wet hats with smiles, and drove off.

"Catch you later, man." Randy shouted from across the street, rubbing the knee he had just scraped on the cement.

Rodney nodded, "Yea bud, much later," and went inside just in time for dinner.

CHAPTER 5
POT ROAST AND INSECT LARVAE

Rodney's mom, carrying the pot roast to the kitchen table, winked at Rodney as he sat in his place in front of the window. Chance, Rodney's sister, sat in her place to the left in front of the kitchen bar. Teresa was her real name, but she lost it one family Monopoly game when with every other roll she landed on a Chance space. "What were the Chances of that?" Rodney joked at the time. Anyway, the joke stuck and from then on everyone called her Chance. She even had some cousins who still didn't know her real name.

Dad dashed in, kissed mom on the cheek, brushed his hand through Chance's hair and squinted into Rodney's face, "You got somethin' in your left eye, son?"

"No dad, mom just didn't see the 'SLOW' sign," Rodney replied.

Anyway, Rodney could have said anything, "No dad, in fact, I lost my whole pupil -- it just rolled right out of my eye like a ball bearing," or "Yes, it's an octopus -- I was in the bath and it just swam right into my eye," or "Sorry dad, these aren't my eyes, I traded with Randy." Rodney's dad didn't really listen for an answer; he sat at his place nearest the TV and turned it on.

"Why do we always gotta watch TV at dinner time?" Chance whined.

"Why shouldn't we watch TV?" Dad defended.

Chance wriggled her head, "My teacher says that families should talk together at dinner and it's a shame that so many families just go ahead and watch TV instead."

"Okay," Dad flicked the set off and turned toward Chance plopping his chin into his hands, "What do you want to talk about?"

Chance shrugged her shoulders desperately trying to think of something to talk about, but nothing came to mind. Dad leaned towards her even more, lifting his eyebrows sarcastically. The room was silent as mom sat and the Appleseed family began to eat completely without sound except for the drops of water from the leaky faucet.

Rodney bit into the end of his piece of pot roast as he studied each drop of water that fell into the sink. Each drop built up slowly on the round edge of the faucet until it could no longer bear its own weight and fell a full ten inches into a coffee cup that had been placed at the bottom of the sink. "What happens to the drop when it hits the cup? Maybe, it completely loses its identity. It surrenders its individuality to become one mass of water the size and shape of the inside of the cup. I wonder if the drop likes that. Maybe it's a better life that way -- bigger, stronger, not so lonely. In that case the drop may dangle above the cup eagerly awaiting enough strength to leap off and add itself to the universe of water below. But, maybe that's not the case at all. It's possible that the drop dreads the idea of losing itself to the greater population. Maybe, it hangs on for its own dear life, but finally cannot bear the weight alone. Perhaps, the drop sees the cup as a kind of dying thing, and jumps in a moment of despair -- maybe the drop couldn't stand the decor of our kitchen. Nonetheless, what's the point of the cup in the first place? Why do people put a cup under a dripping faucet? It doesn't make any sense. The water eventually overflows the cup and proceeds down the drain anyway. Does the cup give the illusion of solving the problem? I don't think so ... "

"Rodney? Rodney lift your head up right now, boy!"

Rodney bobbled his head upward, blurry eyed.

"That's much better. Now, what do you have to say for yourself before I punish you?"

"That I was wrong. I should have respected you. I didn't. I should have at least asked first."

"It would have been nice if you asked first, but I

would have said no, you know."

"Yes Mrs. Finkelstein, I can see why."

"But Rodney, I think we have both learned quite a lot from each other, therefore, I don't think that punishment would be productive. So let's just leave this matter as something in our pasts."

"Sure, I really do feel like I learned something. But what've you learned?"

"I've learned that you don't really hate me, that you're just kids, that I'm much more paranoid than I should be, and that it is mostly my fault that the class and I don't feel so much like friends."

"Woah, you know ... all this learning big stuff ... I feel like we should hug or somethin'."

"Okay then Rodney, give me a hug."

"Mrs. Finkelstein, I kind of liked the feeling of being under hypnoses -- could you do that again?"

"Okay then Rodney, just listen to the water dripping, dripping, dripping, and one more thing Rodney: good shot! Truly an unforgettable shot!"

"Rodney? Rodney lift your head up right now!"

"Oh Geeze, I'm sorry dad."

Dad shook his head, "See, Chance, it's so quiet that your brother fell flat asleep in his mashed potatoes."

"Hey, did you hear about the bull?" Mrs. Appleseed offered up for discussion.

"Yea, yea -- old news," dad responded.

Once again the quiet fell over the Appleseeds' dinner table. Rodney wiped the mash potatoes from his face.

"Did you hear what the Johnsons' found?" Chance blurted out with the excitement of finally finding something to talk about.

"No, Chance, what did the Johnsons' find?" mom responded, happy to have a topic for discussion.

Chance leaned her head over her plate, "Well, I was walking to band practice after school and I overheard Mrs. Soss filling in Mrs. Johnson about what happened on "Murder, She Wrote." And then, and then, Mrs. Johnson started talking about what Mr. Johnson found in the yard in front of Popeye's doghou ... "

"Ice shouldn't float mom!" Rodney interjected, "I'm sure there must be some mistake about that."

"Rodney, your sister was talking," mom reminded.

Rodney apologized and then faded away into thoughts related to changes in states of matter. To the rest of the family, he appeared pretty much like the normal Rodney they usually converse with, except that this Rodney was deaf and blind to them. They couldn't see the deaf part, but they did notice that his eyes weren't focusing on anything in particular and that his foot kept a steady tapping rhythm. Only Rodney, I, and now you, dear reader, know that Rodney wasn't really in that kitchen. Even Rodney couldn't be sure he'd actually left, and certainly any member of his family would tell us that they'd seen him there at the dinner table the whole time. So then, only you and I know for sure that Rodney left the table for a time, and that what the Appleseeds saw was kind of like a shell, like the crusty shell insect larvae leave behind. It looks just like an insect, but if you touch it, it will crumble; break into flakes that blow away in the wind.

"So they brought it inside. The Johnsons did," Chance continued, "They were gonna call an ambulance, but they weren't real sure it was human. Mrs. Johnson said it looked just like the thing in that movie 'The Blob'. So Mr. Johnson went to get a crowbar, since he used his crowbar to fix the toilet when it broke and just about everything else around the house, and why not use it to fix this blob thing, cause it looked like it was all knotted up. So they left it on the coffee table, but when they came back it was gone. Just gone, and there were some kind of seeds all over the place. Mr. Johnson said they should plant them just to see what would grow, but Mrs. Johnson was afraid that they might grow into a whole bunch of blobs so she cleaned them all up and threw them in the garbage disposal."

"You shouldn't discard what you don't understand. Further, how can liquid nitrogen freeze almost anything solid, without being a solid itself?" Rodney spoke as if in a trance. He didn't look at anyone and no one paid any attention to him.

"But," Chance added, "Randy told me that he saw Mr. Johnson planting somethin' in the yard anyway. What do ya think about that?"

"Well, I never thought Bill Johnson's elevator went

to the top floor." Mr. Appleseed said.

"Yea, but just for fun," Mrs. Appleseed proposed, "pretend it really happened -- would you plant the seed or wouldn't you?"

"I would!" Chance bounced.

"Hmmm, well, pretend eh?," Mr. Appleseed let himself pretend, "Okay, let's say it happened right here, right here in our house. Well, why not? The blob didn't hurt anyone -- did it? Everyone seemed quite lighthearted about it. Perhaps we could learn from it."

"That's it dad! Be adventurous," Chance encouraged.

Mrs. Appleseed smiled, "Frank, it's good to see you using your imagination again. Pretend isn't just for kids."

"Suppose we did plant it," Frank Appleseed continued, "and watered it everyday, perhaps in a few months we'd have a blob of our own."

Chance expanded, "Yea, and then in a year or two, it could turn into a person or something."

"Yea, and we could raise it like our own son, and no one on the block would ever know that our son was once a blob and before that some kind of seed -- maybe even an apple seed." Mrs. Appleseed once again giddy, retorted.

"Ha, an apple seed," Mr. Appleseed grinned, "wouldn't that be ironic? How about you, Rodney? What do you think?"

"Rodney?" Frank Appleseed reached over to tap Rodney on the shoulder. What appeared to be Rodney's shoulder tore open like colored paper. The small force of Mr. Appleseed's tap was enough to eventually collapse the entirety of what appeared to be Rodney. The crust cracked, shattered and broke into a hundred weightless flakes that the wind picked up and blew through the window.

"Shining Eye?"

"Shining Eye?"

"Rodney, didn't you hear me calling you?"

"Warm Face!" Rodney popped, "It's so great to see you."

Warm face smiled warmly, "It's grand to see you also. I am sorry I had to pull you from your family so suddenly, but there is someone I want you to meet who will soon wake up, so I had to come get you now."

Rodney scratched his head wondering if he should try to remember whatever it was that he was thinking about, or just forget it all together -- after all, it was so great to see Warm Face again. "So who is this person?"

"His name is Benjamin, but his mother calls him Benj."

"Warm face, that would be so wild to meet Benj. His mother told me a bit about him. But ain't he half way around the world in Thailand or somethin'?"

"Actually, Taiwan. That's why we must go now, because it is nearly morning there and Benjamin will wake soon."

"So why's it so important for you to take me to see him? Am I s'posed to learn more about culture and strange different things?"

"Nope, this time you will do the teaching."

"Me?"

"Shining Eye, do not underestimate your power as a living thinking being. You were smart enough to realize that the world has much to teach you about yourself. But, I'm surprised that you haven't yet realized that you can teach the world much about itself."

"I like that idea."

"Sure, the universe is like a huge light. No one should be afraid to reach out and swallow some. Although, we'd all appreciate it if you'd kindly opened your eyes to us if you did take a gulp, so that we could see some of that warm light inside you."

"Warm face, I think you must have swallowed a lot of light."

"That's sweet, Shining Eye. Now, let's go let your face be warm, for someone who needs a warm face."

"Okay, what should I do?"

"Just be you, don't be shy -- that's like closing your eyes -- he needs to see your eyes. He misses his family and he just feels a little lonely and low in spirit. Cheer him up, give him confidence. Confidence is one of the greatest things you can give to somebody. It's easy to give, but unfortunately, people make accepting it so difficult."

"Okay, let's go."

"All right, Shining Eye, he is currently in the middle

of another dream, let me pull him from that and then I will leave you two alone."

"Goodbye Warm Face, thank you."

CHAPTER 6
SEVENTEEN CONCENTRIC IVORY SPHERES

"Excuse me sir, I believe your name is Benjamin."

"Yea, wow, I just had the weirdest thing happen to me. I was in this elevator that took me down into this strange apartment, totally overflowing with stupid knick knacks, you know, onyx bulls and mahogany Buddhas, all that kind of stuff ... and this big gentle Santa Clause type of guy offers me some honey, but there's bees still in the jar. He can tell that I'm skeptical so he takes a swig of the stuff with the bees still buzzing around in the jar. So I figure, hey, why not? I take a sip and it's the sweetest taste around. And the bees, I can see them lookin' back at me from inside the jar as I sip. They're buzzing past my nose ... it tickles and almost makes the honey taste carbonated."

"Crazed! That *is* pretty weird."

"Then this Santa guy says something like I'm

supposed to go now. Just then one of the bees turns its butt to my face and stings me right on the nose. I break apart like shaved ice cream into a million pieces and the wind takes me here to you."

"I can relate ... to the being blown up part."

"So anyway, how'd you know my name?"

"I met your mom."

"Geeze, my mom, I miss her. How is she?"

"She's doing well, she misses you. I really liked her, Benj."

"Me too! How's she doin'?"

"Well, I don't know what else to tell you 'cept that we sat around talking for a while ... and then we played hopscotch."

"Hopscotch? Really? Wow. I love my mom, even though she can be a little odd at times. So, did she give you anything to give me."

"Confidence and a hug. She didn't specifically tell me to give it to you, but I'm sure she'd want ya to have it."

The two sons leaned open armed in the dream, holding each other as pioneers hold to ideas. Rodney looked Benj square in the face, "Benj it's very important that you plant any seed that finds its way to you."

"Yes sir," Benj grinned with watered eyes, "Thank you."

Rodney could see his own shining eye reflecting in Benjamin's tears. His chest swelled, "I feel like starlight is pumping through my heart instead of blood."

"Hey! Take this," Benj said pulling a whitish ball from his pocket.

Rodney held the ball up to his eyes and looked into it through the many carved holes.

Benj explained, "The old man in the previous dream gave this to me. I've seen balls of this type before at a museum in Taipei. They're from Mainland China. As you can see they are hand-carved out of ivory."

"But it looks like five or six ivory balls carved one inside the other."

"Actually, there's seventeen concentric spheres."

"Seventeen? How'd the carver get 'em inside each other?"

"The carver used only one piece of ivory. First, he cut those delicate designs in the outermost ball and used them as windows to put his tools through to cut the next ball inside the outer one. And then he cut designs in that new ball and again used both design holes to cut the third ball inside and like that."

"That had to take years!"

"Yea, lifetimes maybe."

"You'd think the artist would've been satisfied with three or four concentric spheres, but seventeen ... ?"

"You're right. I'm an artist too; but since I've seen this work, I almost feel like there's no need to create anything more. This is the perfect piece. There's no human creation greater than this," Benj paused in thought and smiled, "well, thanks for stoppin' by, I've gotta wake up now. Bye bye."

"Bye bye," Rodney watched as the small pieces that were Benjamin faded away. Then, he turned his attention once again to the ball and to you, dear reader, "You know, reader, I wish I could hold this ivory ball thing up outta the pages of this book for you to stop and look at for a while. I know you'd think it was the most crazed thing you'd ever seen. I wish you could see the careful detail and sweat that these balls have recorded. I bet that you'd breathe in deep, breathe out and then look at the whole world in a different way. My author would've liked to draw it for you on the opposite page, but he just couldn't 've done it justice."

And since Rodney wasn't just printed words, but an actual living thought in the mind of his author, he looked around his author's mind for some useful information about the ball so that you, dear reader, may have a chance to one day view this magnificent piece, "Oh wow, I can see right out my author's eye. This is amazing! I can watch him typing on a little black computer. It's funny, he can type pretty fast, but he's probably gotta wait for me to speak or think, because that's what he's writing. I can see him writing these exact words," Rodney, paused just for fun -- to see if his author would have to wait for Rodney's next word, but, in fact, the author spent the break writing about the fact that Rodney was pausing. "Well, anyway, I can see around the room my author is in. It's white with a tile floor. There's a mop at the left to spread water on the balcony to keep the place cool. Out the balcony, I see a street quite a distance down, perhaps thirteen or fourteen floors. It looks like a bright sunny day and a breeze is blowing around some lace curtains. I can hear the sound of his fingers typing and Spanish music on a small stereo. There's somebody in the other room cooking, I think, because I can smell some food. There is a painting on the wall that looks like something from Spain. I wonder if we are in Spain? Looking out the window again, this city doesn't look like any city I've ever seen before. My author didn't put his glasses on so it's hard to see details. I'll just look around in his brain -- he must know where he is!"

Rodney started running wild in his author's mind -- like a thought. "Anyway, I'm sure he's gotta be in Spain. It makes perfect sense. It'd explain those Spanish guys in my neighborhood and even maybe that loose bull. Hey! Over here -- some memories. These memories look like they're pretty new cause they're still detailed. I see a stray dog, a taxi, and over there a picture in a newspaper. What a great shot! Some darkly suntanned woman flippin' off this diving platform and in the background you can see the whole city. The pool's gotta be in the mountains! I can even see a real different kind of church -- it's like melting wax. I've seen this church in my geography class. It's in Spain -- I'm sure of it! I just don't remember where. Wow, this is kind of fun searching around in here.

What was I looking for in the first place? Oh yea, that Chinese ball thing. Hmmmm. Oh look, part of this book, it's in my author's memory too. Hey, it looks like my author's been to a lot of countries. There are memories from all over the world. Here it is, here's Taiwan. You know, I wouldn't doubt it, if Benjamin was just kind of like a character reflection of my author. Authors do that sort of thing, you know, I learned it in some writing course I had. Pretty crazed huh? That means I met my own author in a dream -- and I even cheered him up! Wow! Over here I see a bunch of memories of art stuff, some of them are very beautiful: a great bird with crazed eyes, a woodcut of hands playing piano, and all right! The ivory ball! I'll have to follow the paths to other memories. Actually, there are several paths. Which makes sense because each memory reminds him of a bunch of other memories. I need the one with the name of that museum. Excuse me a moment."

Rodney dodged in and out of a complex network of memories woven warmly in the mind of his author, visiting friends, family and a myriad of experiences recorded inside the typing man. In a relatively short amount of time Rodney re-emerged, "Here it is, the best I could do for you, dear reader -- if you really want to see this ivory ball thing, and I really think you should, then go to the National Palace Museum in Taipei. It's in the north part of the city. From the other memories I saw, Taiwan looks like a very interesting place anyway. So go."

And then came the tap on Rodney's shoulder shattering him like an eggshell into infinite space.

"Rodney?"

"Rodney?"

"Rodney, didn't you hear us?"

"Oh, I'm sorry, what's up?" Rodney responded incoherently.

"What do ya think? Should we plant the apple seed or not?" Rodney's dad prodded.

Rodney shook his head in frustration, "Of course! Didn't I just say to plant any seed that comes your way?!!"

"I'm sorry, honey, we must've gotten so involved in our own discussion that we didn't hear you," Mom consoled.

"Anyway, thanks for a lovely meal dear," Mr. Appleseed gave rare recognition. "In fact, thanks for all you do all the time. Forgive me for taking it for granted."

"Well, it's my pleasure, Mr. Appleseed, but I'm not so sure I'll forgive you for taking it for granted," Mrs. Appleseed said strongly, "I may soften up, if I hear more compliments and thank you's."

"Fair enough, young lady!" Frank suavely proposed, "How about I take you to a show this evening, and after that ... who knows? If you play your cards right, you might get lucky ... "

CHAPTER 7
NOTHING HAPPENS

"Rodney, I need you to scrape these dishes -- your sister is gonna wash them. Your father and I are gonna try to catch the 8:00 movie, so you're in charge until we get home." Mom instructed as she wiped her mouth with the napkin and stood.

"How come Rodney never hasta wash dishes?" Chance whined -- and was ignored.

"What movie are you gonna see?" Rodney queried (Rodney loved movies).

"I don't know. Whatever's up."

"Mom, why do people write movies?"

"I don't know, why do people fall in love?"

"Why does ice float?" Rodney continued.

"How come Rodney never hasta wash the dishes?" Chance whined and was again ignored.

"Why do people exist at all?" Rodney's dad rolled

his eyes in play. "Why is there something instead of nothing? Isn't nothing much easier?"

Rodney's mom shrugged, "Why can't we ever get to the movies on time?"

Chance turned to the sink, resigned to her role as the family member most likely to be ignored. Rodney's mom freshened up in the bathroom. Rodney's dad went to look for his watch and his wallet. And Rodney's thoughts sailed into the night sky like soup can projectiles set to flight by a few firecrackers and a pack of wide-eyed neighborhood kids.

"Yea, why should we exist?" Rodney contemplated. "What's the whole point of being born? To stay alive? That just doesn't seem like a good enough reason? To help out the world? But how do you help somethin' that has no known reason for being? Where did the whole world come from? Is it important to know that?"

These were very big questions for a boy Rodney's size. They caused his mind to bump and churn which put him once again in danger of becoming 'the blob'. " ... If there's someone or something that's responsible for all this -- then why's it allowing all the bad things like war and destruction and stuff? And why didn't it tell us what we're s'posed to do with this life? When I buy a model -- I get a set of instructions. Where's the set of instructions for us? There hadda be a first man ever -- so why didn't he tell the next guy where he came from and then that guy could tell the next guy and like that? How could a world be so uncertain of how it started out? Yea! And why does ice float?!"

"Rodney!" Chance shouted, "Look out the window -- there's a rainbow!"

Rodney turned to the window behind them and gazed out glassy-eyed.

Chance was quite right; there was, indeed, a rainbow -- a most awesome rainbow stretching from the railroad tracks that carried the train that shook the old house at night to a place out in the distance where Chance and Rodney had never been before.

"Mom and dad gone yet?" Rodney asked as he stared out the window.

"Yep," Chance put her face against the glass. "Ya think there's really a pot a gold at the other end of rainbows?"

"I don't know, Chance. Maybe when I get a car, I'll take you to the end of one and we'll see what we can find."

"Maybe there's gold or maybe a magic short guy that'd grant us wishes."

"Or maybe there's a very old guy -- over three hundred years old and he's very wise and he has this long winding white beard that he hasn't cut in over a hundred years and he knows all the answers to everyone's questions in all the universe. If he were there Chance, what would you ask?"

"I don' know -- I think I'd rather just get a wish."

"Okay, what would you wish for?"

The rainbow glimmered in the rusty dusk sky. It was

very rare to see a rainbow at this hour. The two cuddled up to the small pane as if it were a fireplace on a cold night.

"A horse maybe."

"Come on, every girl wishes for a horse."

"So what's wrong with that? Anyway, I could also wish for ta play the French horn better. Or to see a shootin' star every night. How about you Rodney? What would you wish for?"

"I'd wish for an old man with a white beard to answer all my questions."

"You're no fun at all, Rodney! Why not ask to be in the next World Series and hit a grand slam? Wouldn't that be more exciting than knowing why ice doesn't sink?"

"Sure it'd be fun to hit a grand slam in the World Series, but I'd rather sit and talk with somebody who knows everything about everything. Because, a grand slam's over in twenty seconds, but knowing things is useful all your life."

"Rodney, you're such an egghead sometimes. You'd hate yourself if you knew everything -- 'cause you wouldn't be able to wonder about things anymore. Didn't you ever stop to think that it might be more fun not knowing why the stupid ice cube floats?"

"Chance, you're becoming more fun to talk to everyday." Rodney smiled as he messed up Chance's hair with a great deal of true affection.

"Shut up!" Chance blurted as she elbowed her older

brother with a great deal of true affection.

And the two fell asleep, cuddled at the kitchen windowsill. The sun set gently and the rainbow dissipated into a rich black night sky.

"The sky looks like a plate of glass, like a huge window, like the times I'd look out my bedroom window and imagine myself a traveler in space. Now, here it is -- my window. My window WAS space. My window WAS the universe," Rodney thunk.

The stars shimmered like metal shavings in oil, like the silver in Rodney's left eye, like the feelings one has after waking from a dream.

Gently, the stars disappeared so that the window became black and the white glow that had licked along the tops of small grains of sand and gravel and roof tops and tree leaves and parked cars had dissolved into black.

"It feels like the end of a movie, like the end of all the greatest movies I'd ever seen. I love movies. I'd love for the sky to become a huge silver screen. I'd lay on my back and let the movie have my mind. I'd open the window and crawl inside the writer. I'd stay there until the music climaxed and the images faded to black like the sky. Completely black. Roll the credits! Roll the credits!"

Rodney yelled out into the sky without reply.

"Wow everything is black! I've never seen anything so black. Is this what nothing is? Completely black nothing's visible. Nothing's everywhere. Nothing is bumping up against my skin and oozing in through my pupils ... Roll the credits! Roll the credits! Who's responsible for all this? Where's those answers everybody talks about?"

The sky gave no response.

"I'm Popeye the sailor man. I'm Popeye the sailor man." Rodney scratched his head, continuing the melody in whistle. An hour passes like a day.

"Roll the credits! Where's those answers?! Roll them like credits!"

Nothing but black replied.

"'White is the presence of all color,' that's what Mrs. Galek said, like a rainbow. And black's the absence of all color. The void. The void. I think that there's a place like this in my body somewhere -- maybe just to the left of my spleen or just below my lungs or something like that. I felt that place when I got picked last for football. I remember, Randy felt it when his big brother got too old to play with him. I felt that place when my best friend moved away. I feel that place whenever I can't make a decision -- like everythin' stops until I decide. It's a place I've always tried to fill with somethin', but it always drains back to nothin' eventually. And now I'm sitting in it -- just to the left of my own spleen possibly. Maybe it's necessary that nothing is a biological part of the body like an appendix. No one knows what it's for, but it just sits there quietly ... maybe even waiting to explode one day."

Rodney sat rich with emotional thoughts, taking full breaths deep within the empty, dark, almost peaceful, nothing.

"In an odd way nothing feels good in my lungs. Hmmm, what if I were to put it in my mind? Would I be able to think again? Maybe it'd be nice to have a rest from thinking. I don't remember ever takin' a rest. In fact, I don't remember any waking minute that I had no thoughts at all! Geeze, I'm always thinking -- just like now! How tiring!"

Rodney tried to let nothing happen in his mind, but it was real hard. Nonetheless, he almost had it to where every time a thought started to enter in his mind -- he'd close the door on it. He imagined himself a boy in a round room with infinitely many doors to it. Every time he heard a knock he'd say "Go away!" And even when some thoughts would knock real hard and jiggle the doorknobs, still Rodney would not allow them in.

"I have closed as many doors as I could, I will now just trust that the thoughts will respect my privacy and not attempt to use the doors that I have not checked. All I have left to do is to shut off the light in this room."

The room was infinite and so it took Rodney a long time to find the light switch. By the time Rodney found it, he was very tired. And just as he flipped it off -- he fell asleep. He dreamed that he was in infinity at night and nothing at all was around except popcorn and this huge silver screen sky. The credits rolled:

FADE TO BLACK:

THE UNIVERSE HAS BEEN A PRESENTATION
OF
ITS PROUD CREATOR
(FILMED ON LOCATION IN INFINITY)

SPECIAL THANKS TO:
MR. AND MRS. JOHNSON
HOGAN
POPEYE
THE BULL
THE BUS DRIVER
MRS. FINKELSTEIN
RODNEY APPLESEED AND HIS MOM
CHANCE APPLESEED AND HER FATHER
INSANITY RANDY
BENJAMIN AND HIS MOTHER
WARM FACE
THE PAMPLONAN
HANES AND BAGGIO
WILL AND THE CARPENTER
PATTY AND HENRY
FIRST SERGEANT EDWARD SANCHEZ
ROCKY
DAN

THE FOLLOWING ANSWERS HAVE MADE
THIS PRESENTATION POSSIBLE:

YES
LIFE HAS A POINT.
NO
YOU PROBABLY WON'T BE TOLD EXACTLY
WHAT IT IS.
BUT
YOU WILL FIND A GREAT MANY HINTS
HERE ARE SOME NOW:

1 THE POINT IS INSIDE YOU,
   JUST AS NOTHING IS.
2 THE UNIVERSE SUPPORTS YOU
   IN YOUR SEARCH FOR IT.
3 DON'T KEEP US WAITING TOO LONG.

AND ONE MORE THING:
EVEN IF EVERYONE TELLS YOU THAT
EVERYTHING CANNOT POSSIBLY GROW FROM
NOTHING,
PLANT A SEED THERE ANYWAY.

CHAPTER 8
WHAT IF A SHOOTING STAR FELL TO EARTH

Rodney smiled in the darkness, flipped the light back on and awoke to that feeling of disappearing stars. He opened his eyes to nothing, scratched a hole in the ground and planted an apple seed anyway.

A figure dissolved in from the darkness.

"Warm Face! I'm happy to see you, but that means I'm in a dream."

"I'm happy to see you and I am happy that it is in a dream that we meet."

Warm Face brushed Rodney's sandy blonde hair away from his forehead so that she could watch his eye shine.

Rodney looked right back up at her (she was a little taller) and watched her face be warm.

They hugged.

They hugged for a long time.

They hugged for probably fifteen minutes. That's a long time for a hug -- especially in a dream.

"It's wonderful to hold you Warm Face. You seem so great to me. I was afraid to touch you."

"Oh? Shining Eye, please don't be afraid of me. You too seem so great to me, how would you feel if I was afraid to touch you?"

"It's hard to imagine that you could think of me the way I think of you. I'm not so great."

"Oh yes you are, Shining Eye. Don't think lowly of yourself -- you would be missing the point completely. I am enjoying holding you just as much as you are enjoying holding me."

"That's incredible! I couldn't have imagined it'd be so wonderful."

"Maybe not imagined, but dreamt it ... certainly!"

"I don't feel like ever letting go Warm Face. I feel so good hugging you this way."

"Thank you. But, how long do you think you could actually hold me?"

"Forever."

"Oh come on, Shining Eye. I am enjoying this too, but forever? Forever is an awfully long time. And not only must you eat and use the bathroom sometimes, but if you didn't go out into the world and be Rodney Appleseed, I don't think I would enjoy these hugs so much. I would hate to have you exist for me. And I would immediately refuse to exist for you. I am Warm

Face and there is so little time for me to do so much as myself. Part of who I am is to hug you like this, but not all and not forever. Please don't feel rejected -- please feel strongly Shining Eye."

"You know, seems like when I just start understanding things, somethin' happens to knock me back to square one."

"And it's all right to feel that way, because you never really go back -- you just get scooted off to the side a bit. You are learning. You really are learning and much faster than most."

"Warm Face, why do people fall in love?"

"Okay, look, I know why I can't hug you forever. But love? I still haven't figured out. If you do, please let me know."

"Warm Face, I almost feel like saying 'I love you,' but I don't really know much about love at all. We didn't study it at school."

"If you feel like saying it -- don't pass up the opportunity. Say it. Don't worry about promises or anything. Just say it if it's how you feel. There will be many times in your life when you won't feel like saying it at all."

"I love you."

"Thank you, Shining Eye. Keep the shine in your eye, and I will love you also. But, it looks like your sister is about to wake up so ... "

"Rodney! Rodney! get your elbow off my leg, we gotta take care of the dishes before mom and dad get home."

"Wow, that's right. Thanks for waking me up," Rodney took one last look out the window and smiled, "you know what Chance?"

"What Rodney?"

"I feel great!"

"Well, great! I'm glad you feel great," Chance said just as Rodney's mom would have said it, "now go scrape the plates so I can wash 'em."

"Alrighty then," Rodney faced the table, collected the plates and brought them to the garbage bag. He picked up a fork and a knife and began scraping the remaining potatoes, pot roast fat and corn from each plate.

Chance watched him from the sink thinking to herself that he really did look happy even though she knew he didn't like to scrape the dishes so much.

Rodney scraped the last few lonely kernels of corn off Chance's plate and faded away to rich farmland.

He turned and ran into the cornfield at the right. The sun wove in and out of the clouds like a glowing yellow bobber wading through blue-green waves alert and anxious to announce the discovery of fish. Like fish, crisp green corn leaves swam in the breeze brushing across Rodney's skin. Fallen husks cluttered the narrow ground between the tall stalks. One slick husk cowered as the bottom of Rodney's shoe appeared from the sky, squished it, and slid off. Rodney landed about 10 feet beyond.

At that point the cornfield gave way to a beautiful garden full of all sorts of flowers and vegetables. The flowers seemed to float up from the ground like bubbles in water. They sway-danced in the wind; red, white, and yellow petals opened to kiss Rodney's face as the wind twirled and dipped them. Furry bumblebees (with honey dripping from their backs) zipped in and out like oregano on pizza. Hummingbirds hovered breathless above ground like hearts in love. Metallic dragonflies bowed in and out of violin string stems.

To the left, fat red tomatoes burped, juicy strawberries giggled, thick orange carrots and white onions slept together under the ground.

"Plants are so beautiful, why should people feel any better about eating plants and not animals?" Rodney thought. "Just 'cause plants don't so often cuddle, and they don't usually cry out when they get cut. I mean, at least animals have a chance to run or bite back. What kind of hunter would track down and kill radishes? Where's the sport in that? It's a massacre plain and simple. Plants gotta have feelings too. Why not? I wonder what it feels like to stand all day in the same place? Sucking from the planet what you need to stay alive. Opening from a seed under the earth and pushing. Pushing through dirt up. How do they know which way is up? Is the ground warmer towards the sun? Is it instinct or faith? Is it just a hunch? Are there just as many that grow down? What's on their minds as they struggle against the mud and gravity in complete darkness? Complete nothing, but weight. Do seeds have any idea of how wonderful the sun is? Alone in that damp black world where insects and germs claw at them all day, what are those seedlings thinking? It'd be so crazed to sit one day and have a long talk with a seedling. And then, geeze! Breaking through that last clot of dark. That first crack of light -- it's gotta be blinding. The weightlessness of the atmosphere hasta be dizzying. The sharpness of all the colors glitterin' in the dew, the massage of a sunshower must feel like a hundred million kittens lickin' your face at the same time."

Rodney reflected like light through rain as the leaves spun in circles around him like kites, like model airplanes. He picked up his feet and stood. Light from the bobbing sun laid patches of bright and shadow across the corn and across the garden like the patches of black and white in the hide of a cow. Out further into the garden Rodney could see a damaged area, nearly round and about eight feet in diameter. Stepping carefully, so that he wouldn't harm the plants, Rodney investigated the problem.

Inside the circle of damage lay dead and suffering plants mangled, broken and covered with dirt. Rodney's Adam's apple hardened and he turned away as the odor of decay reached his nose. Just then, he heard a sound, as if something was moving in that dark circle. Rodney stepped forward into the circle and at its center found a gray rock of some kind rolling back and forth. The rock was about three feet in diameter and by the sound of its movement appeared to weigh as much as a locomotive.

"What is making this rock move around like that?" Rodney thought as he grabbed it with both hands in an attempt to stop its motion. "Geeze, it's cold as steel -- I never seen a rock like this before." Rodney tried, but his efforts had no effect on the phantom boulder. "Innocent plants are being killed by this rock's ignorant wallowing. It seems to have a power all its own, can't it see the beauty it's eclipsing? I wish it would stop moving about! It's so cold! Where did this thing come from? It reminds me of nothing! Could it have fallen from infinity? Maybe it's a part of infinity. Maybe it's part of another planet ... maybe it was a shooting star." Rodney fixed a cold stare on the frigid rock. "My God, I'll bet you were a shooting star! I'll bet you used to soar through the universe like a steel eagle skating across black sandpaper. You must've given us an awesome light show. What was it like to feel the heat of your own glow? What was it like to make hearts flutter like the wings of the night owls? And then to leave a wake of rippling kisses? How hard this planet hadta seem to you as you hit. What a bummer, huh? Now you can't fly freely in a burst of light. And you won't make hearts hover anymore. No wonder you've grown cold."

"But, you know, you're killing these plants. You're

ignoring a different kind of wonder. There's seeds all around you that'd like to have a chance to see the sun. Plants got the beauty of shooting stars too, you know, but they just spread it out a little thinner over time. Thanks cold rock, for even once shootin' arrows of awe into an occasionally apathetic, universe. But you gotta stop your thrashin' about. There's seeds all around here. I wish you'd open up your eyes and feel them. If you'd just stop wallowing in your own weight, you'd see that you're sitting in the middle of a beautiful garden! Don't you like the scent of flowers? You know, some plants around here might just warm you up a bit -- you're as cold as a refrigerator with a burnt out light."

Two sparrows passed by. A squirrel ran between trees. The rock rolled over once and did not move again.

"Rodney? Rodney, you stopped moving."

"I what?"

"You stopped moving. You're just standin' there. Now give me that last plate so I can wash it and be done."

"Yea sure, sorry Chance."

"Hey, you want to play a game or something after we finish?"

"like what?"

"Like 'War' or 'Monopoly' or just draw."

"How about 'What If ... '?"

"What's 'What If ... '?"

"'What If ... ' is a game we used to play in Ms.

Sampler's class."

"I never had Sampler. I got stuck with Bosler."

"Geeze yea, sorry about that. Anyway, the game goes like this ... Someone picks a topic and then they or maybe another person makes a 'What If ... ' statement about it."

"Okay, but after that let's play a mindless game of 'War'."

"It's a deal!"

"So it's your game -- you pick a topic."

"All right, let's see. Hmmmm. Elevators!"

"Elevators? Okay, what if ... what if elevators were never invented?"

"Yea, Good Chance. Then all those business men in their three piece suits would get all sweaty climbing the stairs all day."

"Yea so, maybe their bosses would let 'em wear bathing suits to work and maybe they'd have pools on every floor too! ... "

" ... And insteada pools maybe each employee's work space'd be a large bath, so that the person would be sitting at his desk in a cool tub of water ... "

" ... And then they'd haveta come home to their families all wrinkled up -- like prunes."

" ... And somebody would have to invent a kind of paper that wouldn't get messed up by the water."

"Yea Rodney! And if they did a good job their bosses could give 'em rubber duckies."

"But if there were pools on every floor, the

buildings would be so heavy that maybe they would sink into the ground."

" ... Sink so far that the people on the top floor could just walk right out of the building onto the street."

"Okay, there's an idea ... so someone figures out a way to make the whole building go up and down so that people on any floor could get out onto the street and enter again at any floor."

"So you wouldn't need an elevator, 'cause the whole building would go up and down."

"That's right, but every one's baths might spill over if the building moved too fast."

"And some people might have stomach problems."

"Good point, Chance. Besides, you'd have to wait twice to get to the floor you wanted. I mean, if you were on the 17th floor and you wanted to go to the 31st floor, you'd first have to wait until the 17th floor stopped at street level, then get out and wait again until the 31st floor stopped at street level."

"It's better than walking, but it's still not as good as an elevator."

"Also, it would be much more difficult to make the building go up and down than to just make a box go up and down. So, Chance, you're right. I think the elevator is a better solution."

"Hey that was fun. I didn't think it was going to be, but it was."

"Told you."

"Even though I knew from school that before there were elevators there were only short buildings."

"Ah, I didn't even think about that. You know, it seems that all my ideas have been limited by the little bits of the world that I have been able to see or read about. I didn't even consider -- not having tall buildings."

"Yea, it was in some social studies book. Someone finally invented the elevator sometime after 1850 -- I don't remember exactly. Anyway, they were finally able to build the tall buildings. They knew how to make tall buildings already, Mr. Sharky said, but I guess they thought about sweaty businessmen like we did and decided no one'd want a building like that so they just didn't make 'em."

"Until, the elevator came along ... "

"Yep!"

"It hadta be frustrating for the architects who knew how to make the tall buildings."

"Yea, they'd haveta just sit around and wait for the elevator inventor."

"Could they've done anything else? I mean, to just sit on a good idea waiting for technology must be depressing."

"Maybe they coulda done time travel -- like in the movies and come back with knowledge of elevators? Even talk with the inventor himself?"

"But that wouldn't make any sense, Chance, 'cause if they could go into the future a hundred years, let's say, and talk with the inventor of the elevator, then probably there'd already be a lot of tall buildings with elevators before 1850. Therefore, the elevator inventor wouldn't have existed -- because there'd have been no need for an inventor -- 'cause elevators woulda already been common. And if the inventor didn't exist, then the architects couldn'ta met him even if they time-traveled."

"But, maybe just one architect went into the future and he made just one tall building, just for his family and uncles and grammas and cousins. And the building had only one room on each floor -- just to do it."

"I see your point. A very tall narrow house/building maybe twenty-seven or twenty-eight stories high. One room per floor per person."

"And a den for the dad and a toy room for the kids on the top floor."

"And a recreation room with a Ping-Pong table ... "

"Rodney, when was Ping-Pong invented?"

"And a library ... "

"And a music room with a piano and every instrument ever."

"And they put an elevator on the side of it and no one in the whole clan ever told anybody about it. So that history wouldn't be messed up. And, of course, the guests'd understand that so they wouldn't speak about it either."

"And on the other side of the building they put a fireman's pole, so you'd just slide down instead of waiting for the elevator."

"Yea, and because the architect mighta built this before electricity was discovered, he'd haveta attach the elevator to a horse or somethin'."

"Maybe by just a rope, so if you put some food thirty feet away from the horse, he'd pull you thirty feet up the side of the building."

"Ingenious Chance! So they'd have a marker laid on the ground duplicating the distances to each floor."

"I like it!"

"I like it, too! So, little sister, you have enlightened me. Time travel is okay as long as you are the only one who uses the ideas you learned from the future!"

"And keep it a secret!"

"Crazed!"

"Okay, are we done?"

"I suppose so."

"Well Rodney, you promised a game that didn't require thinking. You promised a game of odds alone."

" ... A game of complete CHANCE!"

"Very funny." Chance snipped, glaring at him while curling her nose a little bit, "a relaxing game of 'War'."

"'War' it is then -- cut the deck and prepare to be beaten!"

The two siblings pulled a deck of forty-eight cards from the junk draw and sat on the rug in the front room. Chance shuffled and dealt from the bottom of the deck. Rodney's high cards were met nearly each time with a card one higher, by chance, until ... "War!" Chance grunted. The two twos lay on the carpeting.

"One under, one over ... now!"

Rodney flipped his four over to Chance's six.

"Chance, you got my king. I give up. I don't have any more power cards."

"No! You have to sit there and play until I win each and every one o' your cards."

"That's the way it is in real war too, I'll bet."

"If you lose, you lose everythin'."

"Why do countries have wars?"

"I don't know. Dad says all wars are over money or power. I think it's so stupid."

"Mr. Sharky says it's population control."

"I mean, life is pretty much fun isn't it?"

"Yea, I s'pose."

"And you and me Chance, we don't have any money."

"And definitely not power."

"And we still are enjoying ourselves. So why would anybody want to kill somebody else just for money or power?"

"Or population control?"

"I don't think people fight for population control, it's just something that happens as a result."

"Gottcha. Anyway, you're getting all worked up, this was s'posed to be a relaxing game. Okay, let's quit. You lost, so you gotta pick up the cards. I'm gonna go watch 'Pokemon'."

"Oh, that'll be mindless for sure," Rodney picked

up all forty-seven cards and placed them neatly into the faded box. A knock came at the door.

CHAPTER 9
WAR AND PEACHES

"I'll get it," Rodney mumbled.

"Who is it?" Rodney yelled through the door. He leaned against it for a reply.

But instead of a reply, the door burst off its hinges, sending Rodney to the floor -- the cracked door landing on top of him. Loose nails and splinters of wood bounced along the floor clouding the room with dust. Chance ran and hid in the pantry between the coffee cans and the chimneystack. Rodney lifted the door just a bit from his belly and peaked from underneath to see a very large young man in military uniform with a big gun and a head full of sweat -- so much that he looked like he had taken a shower in his uniform and everything.

"First Sergeant, Edward Sanchez, US National Guard -- If you have any food or drink, you are required by the United States Government to surrender it to me now," The exhausted soldier commanded.

Rodney froze, clinging to the door. The dust continued to settle, First Sergeant Sanchez pulled the door from Rodney's clutch, placed it back in the doorway, and stepped swiftly to the kitchen. Sanchez pulled some apple juice from the refrigerator and then moved to the pantry for bread. Chance's eyes enlarged as the soldier's filthy boots brushed against her side. He was grunting and spilling the juice as he poured it into his face, still searching for more things to eat. He rolled several peaches out onto the kitchen floor by the sink, shut the window nearest Rodney's place at the table and drew the curtains in nearly one motion.

Rodney slowly brought himself to his feet, stepped carefully to the front door and once again peeked from its side, this time out into the street. To his surprise, tanks were rolling across lawns, men in uniform were hiding in stairwells and helicopters shining bright cones of light, buzzed only one hundred feet above the ground. Rodney ran to the kitchen.

Edward Sanchez sat on the floor in front of the sink staring blankly at the stove in front of him, peach juice drooled down his neck. Rodney watched him devour three peaches in less than a minute.

"We got some bananas too." Rodney offered.

Sanchez didn't respond, he just kept chewing and drinking until he had finished all that he had rolled out for himself on the floor. After a long deep sigh, his head dropped onto his knees and he fell fast asleep.

Chance crawled quietly from the pantry, "Rodney! It's a soldier, a real soldier, and he's made a mess of the place just after we finished cleaning it up. Mom's gonna kill him."

"I think mom is the least of his problems," Rodney replied.

"Anyway, what should we do with him?"

"You mean pull his gun away and shoot him?"

"I don't know."

"Don't be silly, he's on our side. Plus, he didn't seem too much interested in us -- just hungry and tired."

"How long do ya think he'll sleep?"

"I don't know, Chance."

"He looks so peaceful for a soldier. I wonder if he's dreaming?"

"Yea, and if so, about what?"

"Maybe he's dreaming of a beautiful woman."

"Perhaps, a tall girl with straight black hair and a red tint in her dark skin," Rodney crept up close to him and stared into the soldier's heavily closed eye.

"Rodney, careful. You'll wake him."

"Look at him, Chance, he's so peaceful now; moments ago he was breaking things and sweating and now he's so calm. I'm sure he's dreaming of a warm face."

Chance moved in closer as well and Rodney held his hands around the sleeping soldier's head in an attempt to feel his dreams.

"Do you suppose people give out some kind of energy when they're dreaming?" Rodney whispered.

"I don't know," Chance's curiosity grew, "What do you feel, Rodney?"

Rodney's palms hovered on either side of Sanchez's ears, "I feel the heat from his body. That's all I can feel. I want to feel more. I want to reach into his head and grab his dream like a cat grabs a fish out of a fishbowl."

"Whoa, nice analogy." Chance noted.

"Warm Face? Are you in there, Warm Face?" Rodney leaned his ear to the man's head, "I miss you," and Rodney kissed Edward's forehead.

"Rodney!!!!????" Chance shuttered. "What are you doing?"

"I'm sorry, Chance. I don't feel anything except the heat from his body. Do you see anything?"

"Yea, I see dried blood all over his clothes."

"Do you s'pose he's injured?"

"He didn't seem injured?"

"Yea, but sometimes people go into shock or get this amazing boost of adrenaline that lets 'em act like they're okay. I saw it in a movie once."

Just then the soldier coughed; the two siblings jumped back against the stove. Eyes still shut, the soldier raised his head up until it faced Rodney and Chance, both of whom sat open-jawed only a few feet away. Slowly, Edward's eyelids lifted like rusted garage doors -- his face expressionless, his eyes on

Rodney.

"Did you just kiss me?" First Sergeant Edward Sanchez asked.

Rodney stuttered, "Well, I ... I ... "

"He did! I watched him do it," Chance reported.

Sanchez lazily drifted his eyes to Chance and then began to roll his head on his stiff neck, "What's your name kid?"

"I'm Rodney and this's my sister Teresa. Sir, if you don't mind me askin', what were you dreaming?"

The soldier smiled and almost chuckled, "I don't know," he shook his head and looked down, "wait ... I was in a huge apple orchard and this old wrinkled farmer came to me. He put his arm around me and kissed me on the forehead."

The three sat quiet for nearly a minute.

Chance, looking concerned, broke the eerie silence, "Are you injured sir?"

"What? ... Oh ... " Edward looked down at his blood stained uniform, "I don't think so," he said as he began checking his abdomen with his hands.

"Then why all the blood?" Rodney asked hesitantly.

"My friends." Edward Sanchez once again dropped his head to his knees, but instead of sleeping, he began to cry.

Chance got up, walked over to the weeping man and kissed him on his forehead also, "You can stay here tonight. Why don't you go ahead and take a shower? you look very tired."

"Yes ma'am, thank you," He replied, wiping his eyes with his sleeves.

Rodney studied the man, "War is so ugly. I want to stop it. I really hate it. But it's so much bigger than me. When I try to even understand it, I just end up feeling overwhelmed and depressed."

"Rodney," Edward answered, "it's true that war is bigger than us both. But don't be too overwhelmed. The world still needs every small contribution towards a peaceful solution. Even if it's as simple as your naive statement that war is ugly." The soldier paused to the sound of the leaky faucet overhead, "Small drops of water will eventually make an ocean. We need you Rodney, use your mind for good. Put positive ideas into the world. There is already so much bad. We need you to put good out there."

The worn soldier stood to his feet and stripped himself naked, "Which way to the shower, Ms. Teresa?"

Chance blinked once nervously and dropped her eyes quickly towards her feet. With her head down she pointed with her index finger, "Upstairs, first door on the right."

Edward made his way up the carpeted stairs, turned right and said in surprise, "This shower is occupied!"

"Oh, I am done sir," a young woman's voice replied. The woman squeezed past the clothesless man in the narrow hallway and stepped downstairs to see Shining Eye.

"Warm Face!" Rodney jumped, "I'm happy to see you as ever, but even more glad that this is a dream."

"It's just a dream for you, Shining Eye, but it is all too real for many many others." Warm Face stated bluntly. "In fact, Edward is a real soldier sleeping in his trench in another country right now. I brought him here because you two would benefit from each other's presence this night."

"Thank you, Warm Face, I learned a lot." Rodney gazed.

"Well Rodney?" Chance tugged at Rodney's shirt.

"Oh ... right! Chance, this is Warm Face. Warm Face, this is my little sister Chance."

Warm Face bowed cordially, "Pleased to meet you, Chance."

"Me too," Chance replied. Sensing that about-to-be-ignored feeling, she turned toward Rodney, "Is she why you were feeling 'great'?" Chance didn't wait for an answer, instead she politely stepped out, "never mind, I'll go clean the front hall."

"Warm Face, I have an idea -- a small contribution, but I don't have the technology to perform the idea. Would it be possible? What I mean is ... " Rodney tilted his head and squinted as if he might have been asking too much, " ... could you take me into the future?"

Warm Face brushed her hand through her long black hair, "The future?"

"Yea, I won't tell anybody what I learn there -- I

promise."

"Shining Eye, you are so very funny. I am a weaver of dreams -- not a time-traveler. So, I am sorry, but I cannot carry you into the future."

Rodney lowered his head.

"However, I can bring the future to you -- sort of."

Shining Eye raised his head.

"I have a friend that lives in a place where he can see all of time all at once."

"Wow! all of time all at once!"

"It is a lot to see and if you weren't born there it might make you insane. But my friend's family has lived there for generations and they are not only used to it, but can even make sense of it from time to time."

"I can't even begin to imagine seeing all of history and present and future at the same time."

"Wait here, Shining Eye, he's sleeping now -- I'll go get him."

Warm Face dissolved off into space and in almost no time at all another figure dissolved back where she stood in Rodney's kitchen.

"Hogan!"

"Rodney, don't get too excited. I'm not real this time. I'm a dream."

"You're real! You're real!"

"So this is finity?"

"Yea, what do ya think?"

"Pretty small. Don't you feel claustrophobic here?"

"No. Actually it seems quite large to me. I have only

seen such a tiny piece of it."

"I have seen this planet in its entirety from its formation, through its civilizations to its ultimate destruction."

"Its ultimate destruction!?!?!"

"Certainly. Don't be alarmed. All planets are destroyed when their suns ultimately burn out in a supernova. It's an amazing sight -- much better than a history full of Fourth of July's all on one night."

"I didn't know about that."

"I wouldn't worry about it if I were you, you have a relatively young sun. Many of the stars you see in the sky have burnt out already, but you still see them because they are so far away that the light they emitted even ten and twenty thousand years ago is still traveling through space to your eye."

"Wow! Will we learn this in the future?"

"This is not news. Your time knows this. Take an astronomy class in college -- you'll eat this stuff up."

"Hogan, I want to thank you for all you have taught me, I really appreciate it all; and yet I need to ask one more thing."

"That's what Warm Face brought me here for, so speak up Rodney -- ask. By the way, I think she likes you."

"Really?"

"Really."

"I really like her too."

"Really?"

"Really."

"Okay boy, enough of this kid's stuff I've got to wake up soon, I can barely keep my eyes shut. What is it you need to know for your small contribution of good to the universe?" (Hogan knew what Rodney wanted to ask, but letting him ask the questions himself would be useful practice. Infinite beings are well aware of the need finite beings have for practice.)

"I want to send something on the ground out into space."

"You mean a car? An apple seed? Your little sister? What?"

"A shooting star."

"A shooting star? They're usually already in space, you know."

"Not this one. This one crashed into my planet."

"Wow, that's really hard to do. I mean the chances of that are very slim. There's almost infinitely more space out there than there is stuff to crash into."

"So how is it done? What's the technology so that I can do it without calling NASA?"

"Launching a fairly small object into space ... Hmmm ... they could do it now. NASA could, but they are so messy and wasteful at this stage. In a hundred years, you will have the necessary inventions to do it in your own back yard. Unfortunately, these inventions are not as simple as the elevator deal, and I think that it wouldn't be very useful to describe them to you in detail. You'd never be able to get all the parts."

"That's disappointing."

"Rodney, don't be disappointed -- ask me if there's another way."

"Hogan?"

"Yes ... ?"

"Is there another way?"

"Hey, funny you should ask ... in about sixty years the nearest life form to Earth will have discovered a way to knock things off of other planets into space using air currents. I've seen it. It's pretty wild. They create a kind of huge golf club of air and swing it using the magnetic power of black holes."

"So how does that help us now?"

"Now? Now is a word that means so much to you finite people. Patience, Rodney. Shooting stars ride the skies for eons, sometimes even for infinity. Do you know how quickly sixty years passes for the near infinite?"

Rodney shook his head.

"It's a nickel in the parking meter compared to the life of your planet. It's the time it takes lightening to touch the Earth from the sky. And for me, it doesn't mean anything. It appears to be done the second it begins. I can see both ends at the same time."

"Okay, Okay. So I should just wait till I'm in my seventies and then hope that some aliens somewhere will putt this fallen star right off my planet with some kind of wind sling?"

"Look... I know a lot of people in infinitely many

places. I'll see what I can do. But you need to do something now -- while you're still young and inspired to correct this situation."

"What's that, Hogan?"

"You know, it's much easier to club a golf ball when it's on a tee ... "

"Are you saying I've got to hold this massive thing above the ground?"

"I'm saying you've got to find a way to get that thing at least ten feet above the earth and keep it there for twenty-four hours sixty years from now."

"Hogan, I've played golf before and I've made a mess of the lawn trying to hit that ball -- even when it's on a tee. The star is sitting in the middle of a beautiful garden. I wouldn't want the garden to be harmed."

"Very thoughtful of you Rodney, in that case, you must raise that thing twenty-five feet from the ground. Any lower and it gets risky for the garden."

"Okay Hogan, talk with your friends. But if the rock isn't quite twenty-five feet, please don't have them do it."

"No problem."

"No problem for you. But I've got to think of a way to get that massive stone to hover above the ground for sixty years."

"I have faith in you Rodney, consider all your resources. Anyway, I can feel the dawn in my eyes -- I'm beginning to wake up."

"One last thing Hogan ... what's it like to see all of

time all at once?"

Warm Face peeked at Rodney from behind Hogan. She smiled and lifted her finger to tap the infinite being on his shoulder. "It's like a rainbow," Hogan said with a smile as he burst into a million pieces.

CHAPTER 10
FOUR!

Rodney bent his knees and sat cross-legged on the floor thinking.

"Go Rodney! Think Shining Eye! You can do it! Rah Rah Rodney!" Warm Face half-joked, "Give me an 'R'! Give me an 'O'! Give me a ... "

"Give me a hug." Rodney finished.

Warm face stopped her cheerleading, smiled and gave Shining Eye another big long hug. All the while Rodney pondered. All was silent except for Chance's occasional cleaning sounds and the drops from the kitchen sink.

"I could ... no. We could try ... no. Hmmm," Rodney deliberated for quite a while. Warm Face had to keep pulling his hands out of his ears and push his legs away from his mouth occasionally so that he wouldn't become the Rodney blob again.

"Hmmmm. Think golf. Like as in golf club. As in green grass and eighteen holes. Why eighteen? Why not twenty or fifteen? And why do they yell 'FOUR!'? Why don't they just yell 'DUCK!'? Why do they yell 'DUCK!' anyway? Maybe 'cause when they hunt ducks with guns they don't want to hit the other guys when they sight a duck? But 'FOUR'? Why 'FOUR'? Or is it 'FOR'? Maybe way back in the beginning of golf there was this bunch of witch doctors that went golfing on a Wednesday and one of them hit the group of politicians in front of them. Yea, maybe the doctors hit them three times in a row and finally thought to warn them about the next one?"

"FOUR!"

But the warning came too late; the ball had already clunked Rodney right in the head. Rodney lost consciousness for a few minutes just after he hit the ground.

"I'm sorry kid. Didn't you hear me?" a man in plaid pants shouted as he ran up to Rodney's motionless body. "Kid! Geeze, I must have whacked you right in the head," the man knelt checking Rodney for a pulse. Pulling a portable phone from his sports jacket, the man frantically dialed zero.

"So why is it 'FOUR'?" although Rodney's body was down for the count -- his brain was still counting, "and why is it ZERO for operator. Doesn't operator start with 'O' not '0'? And why doesn't '1' have any letters for it on the phone? That really bothers me. I always wanted ta make a word for my phone number, like they do on commercials. Something like 'C-A-R-P-E-T-S' or 'C-O-S-T-L-O-W'. But my phone number has two '1's in it. What am I s'posed to do with '1's? And then you go dialing ZERO for the operator. It just don't figure!"

"Yes, this is the operator. How can I help you?" the small voice from the small phone answered.

"I need an ambulance," the man in plaid pleaded, "I struck a boy with my golf ball."

"Didn't you yell 'FOUR'?" the operator asked?

"Yes, yes of course. 'Could you please just get an ambulance here!?"

"Calm down sir, where are you?"

"I'm out here just about in the middle of his dream."

"His current dream?"

"No, no. The one just before I hit him in the head."

"Okay, I'll arrange for someone to be there right away."

"Thank you. Please hurry."

"I'll do what I can, but we have been experiencing some difficulties with the switchers. We have lines all over the world that are quite vulnerable to acts of God. In fact, there's been some rumors that He has been leaving His number in phone booths around the country ... He must have some long distance bill ... !"

The man put his hand on Rodney's forehead as he hung up the phone. Out from the distance a carpenter drove a pickup toward the two in the field.

The carpenter seemed to understand the situation, and without conversation pulled a six-foot maple one-by-eight from the back of his truck. He laid the piece of wood alongside Rodney. "There are no ambulances in this part of his dream. We're going to have to take him to another dream," The carpenter informed the man in plaid.

The two carefully slid Rodney onto the makeshift stretcher. They lifted him in unison. Rodney rubbed the top of his head and woke up.

"Will Smith!" Rodney shouted, stunned to see Will Smith in his dream.

"Yea, well, look, I did yell 'FOUR'." Will said.

"We were going to take you to get help," the carpenter explained, "but as long as you're okay, I'll just be on my way."

Rodney rolled off the board with a contemplative look on his face and distantly mumbled "Thank you."

"No. Thank *you*, Rodney." The carpenter returned strongly.

Rodney looked back up at him. The carpenter was a big man with sawdust in his hair and the scent of wood in his clothing. Rodney watched the careful way he restacked the plank onto the truck. Will apologized one more time, picked up his ball and returned to the game. Rodney just stood in admiration of the carpenter, watching the truck drive slowly off the curve of his dream into the whited distance.

The sky was nearly silent except for a faint call,

"FOUR!"

Once again Rodney fell to the ground unconscious. But this time he woke up with an idea.

"All right! I got a plan!" Shining Eye stood, left eye shining, right hand rubbing the two bumps on his head.

Warm Face smiled, cheeks warm, "Great! Can I help?"

"Yes, I'll need -- actually I don't need him, I just want him."

"Who?"

"One of those guys I met in the elevator just after school."

"One of the guys in the red armor?"

"Yes. Can you get me one?"

"I can only get him if he's sleeping -- and he's not. Sorry. But, again, I have an alternative."

"An alternative?"

"Sure. You get him. He should be in your author's mind."

"Yea! Right! I can go into my author's memory and find the first section of the book and instead of leaving those guys in the elevator I can ask one to come with me. It's like time travel!"

"No. No. It's not time travel, because you are not going back into time. Everything you're doing will be in the present. You will just be using your author's mind as a way of forcing nearly the same thing to happen twice. It's much more like remembering. Or I might be biased in saying this -- but it's more like your causing your author to daydream."

"Crazed! How do I get back into my author's mind?"

"Just as I am in yours with you -- you are in his with him."

"How cozy."

"Follow your way back through the story in his memory until you find the place where you met those guys in the elevator."

"All right then. Here I go. Hey, Warm Face, could you please meet me in the part of the story where I discover that rock bouncing around in that big beautiful garden?"

"Sure, I like that part. Besides I'm eager to see your plan, Shining Eye."

Shining Eye took a deep breath and then ran as fast as he could backwards through his own story ... yrots nwo sih hguorht sdrawkcab dluoc eh sa tsaf sa nar neht dna htaerb peed a koot eyE gninihS...   ...guh a em eviG...   ...emit emas eht ta sdne htob ees nac I...   ...fo tros -- uoy ot erutuf eht gnirb nac I...   ...dlrow eht ni saedi evitisop htrof tup...   ...oot sananab emos tog ew...   ...?detnevni reven erew srotavele...fi tahw, yakO ?srotavelE...   ...gniyzzid eb tsum erehpsomta eht fo ssensselthgiew ehT...   ...setalp eht eparcs og won...   ...uoy evol I...   ...YAWYNA EREHT DEES A TNALP...   ...deilper kcalb tub gnihtoN...   ...esroh a rof sehsiw lrig yreve ,no emoC...   ...?nrob gnieb fo tniop elohw eht s'tahW...   ...detnarg rof ti gnikat rof em evigrof...   ...gniht llab esenihc taht ,haey

hO... ...yaw wen a ni dlrow nwo ruoy ta kool
neht... ...hctocspoh deyalp neht dna emit trohs a rof
deklat dna tas ew... ...wodniw eht hguorht welb dna
pu dekcip dniw eht taht sekalf sselthgiew derdnuh a
otni ekorb dna... ...dnatsrednu t'nod uoy tahw dracsid
t'ndluohs uoY... ...!mom taolf t'ndluohs ecI... ...?taht
fo secnahC eht erew tahW... ...ylecin deksa
ew ,sediseb dna ,sreganeet diputs tsuj er'eW .taht dias
evah t'ndluoc yeht ,oN ,oN... ...esoh retaw eht htiw
gnilddif elihw redluohs sih revo kcab dellac
ydnaR... ...daeherof s'yendoR dessik dna rac eht otni
daeh reh dewob lrig naidnI eht dnA... ...odnerpmoc
oN ?seuQ... thgil der a ta pots ot ton yako eb lliw ti
taht kniht uoy od... ...eye eulb eno htiw dehgual
yendoR... ...?uoy evah -- gnitnalp eht ni ylpmis yoj
eht nettogrof t'nevah I esuaceB... ...! laer eb em gnittel
rof uoy knahT... ...ytinifni semoceb gnihtyreve ,liaf
tuohtiw dna ,gnihtyreve semoceb gnihton ,nwad
ta ,yllautneve esuaceb... ...EKOMS OTNI EVIRD
T'NOD... ...!eulb ykS 8,7,6,5,4,3,2,1... ...'nilA' ni
ekil -- tuo sedisni eht morf pu uoy tae lliw regna ruoy
yademoS... ...oot delims revird ehT... ...yendoR won
saw taht llab llams eht pu dekcip... ...roloc rehtona
romra ruoy tniap dlouc uoY ...

"Ah, there it is, I passed it up a little."

"That would be a good idea. We didn't think of
that," they nodded affirmingly and raised their
eyebrows at each other.

Rodney continued the thought, "However, you

would still be imprisoned in those metal garments."

Still nodding, "Yes, it does impede our movement a bit."

Confused with another thought, Rodney inquired as politely as he could, "Ahhhemm, by the way, why did you pick red?"

Several responses jumped about the elevator, but Rodney could only catch a few: "It was cheaper", "It goes well with my tie." and "It's my favorite color."

"Other side: Safety and Household Appliances," the fenceman announced.

The elevator stopped, the fenceman politely pressed the DOOR OPEN button, and Rodney stepped out turning to ask the now quiet group of red armor-wearing elevator passengers one last question, "Would one of you like to come with me?"

"Where are you going?" The group said in unison with fear and excitement in their voices.

"I'm going to jump ahead in the story, nearer to the end, so that I can make a small positive contribution to the universe. Would one of you like to come?" Rodney stated plainly.

"Whoa, heavy stuff," one of them remarked. "Are there bulls involved?" another asked wearily.

"Hopefully, just one." Rodney answered, "that's why I need one of you."

The group mumbled among themselves. The fenceman sighed and changed fingers on the door open button.

"I'll go," a tired-eyed man in his forties stepped forward.

"Good for you, sir," Rodney held out his hand, "I'm Rodney. What's your name?"

"Dan," Dan replied as he shook Rodney's hand and stepped out of the elevator for the first time in seventeen years. The others shook their heads in disapproval as the doors came together.

"How does it feel to be out of the elevator after all that time?"

"Like wings must feel to birds."

"Whoa, nice analogy," Rodney noted, "let's go."

"Okay then, I'm following you."

Dan drifted alongside Rodney in amazement as he watched things happen before his eyes in fast forward, "Yea! That's a good question -- why does ice float?"

Rodney was working the new plan out in his head so he really didn't hear much of Dan's comments.

"Don't drive into Jellyfish? What kind of story is this?" Dan could only pick up pieces because the pace of the story appeared to be increased to about ten times its normal telling speed. Actually, the story wasn't moving (like the sun doesn't move) it was he and Rodney that were revolving around it.

Dan looked into Rodney's eyes, "So that's why you got those shavings in your eye! ... Bulls! Oh geeze, look at those guys run! ... You crazy kids. You're lucky those cops didn't try to hit you ... That looks like fun, but I'd never do it ... Wow! I like that part where you just bust up into a million pieces of dust. What did that feel like? ... Heavy stuff, there you are in your author's mind winging past yourself in your author's mind. Wild ... I like your family. I always wanted to have a family ... Yea! Why do we exist? I don't think it's to sit in an elevator. Thanks for coming back in the story for me ... Nice rainbow. I wish we could pause ... Yea, I think I'd take that ... a grand slam in the world series, that'd be pretty remarkable ... Ah, life has a point. I knew it! ... Cute girl, Rodney, I think she likes you, really."

Rodney smiled, "Really?"

"Really." Dan continued his play by playback, "what's that big thing in the garden?"

"That's it. We stop here." Rodney grabbed Dan by the hand and the story slowed to its usual pace.

Dan watched Rodney meld into himself talking, " ... you'd just stop wallowing in your own weight, you'd see that you're sitting in the middle of a beautiful garden! Don't you like the scent of flowers? You know, some plants around here might just warm you up a bit -- you're as cold as a refrigerator with a burnt out light."

Two sparrows passed by. A squirrel ran between trees. The rock rolled over once and did not move again.

CHAPTER 11
A FLY IN THE EAR

"Shining Eye! You did it! You got him!" Warm Face sparked.

Rodney smiled proudly, "Warm Face, this is Dan. Dan, Warm Face."

Warm Face warmly greeted Dan, "Good to have you here in this part of the story."

"Yea, well, it's good to see you for more than half a second," Dan replied. "So Rodney, why am I here?"

Rodney turned knowingly toward Dan, "That's a big question. You'll have to find that out for yourself sometime. But for now I just need you to stand here and attract the bull."

"What?!?!"

"Here, take these apple seeds in your hand, hold them out as if you were offering them to Warm Face," Rodney instructed, "good, now just stand there and be red."

Dragonflies darted, toads croaked, flowers swayed in the wind and Dan Freedman stood shivering, "Uhm, Rodney, and when this bull comes am I supposed to feed him the apple seeds and pet him like a puppy dog or something?"

"Something like that would be fine." Rodney answered.

"And why shouldn't the bull just charge right into me? Or you or Warm Face?" Dan proposed.

"You are wearing sixty pounds of armor, so why should you worry? Stop showing your fear and the bull will respect that. Besides, if you really want me to, I can take you back to the elevator." Rodney was a little surprised to be talking with such confidence. But then again, next to Dan (in his current state), even a mouse would look confident, "We need the bull. We need his strength. And it is important that you make friends with the bull, Dan. I could have gotten a red cape or something, but I wanted you. You can do it. You can make friends with the bull."

Dan considered that elevator return option for several moments and then finally shook his head in disapproval, "I'm here, Rodney. I will make friends with the bull."

Birds could be heard peeping in the nearby trees, the breeze was gentle and cool, and out from between two hills in the distance a single bull could be seen charging towards the garden.

Dan held his breath. Warm Face smiled in excitement. And Rodney pretended that the bull itself was a shooting star -- a red smear across green skies. Instead, a small fly flew into Rodney's ear and disturbed his imagination.

"Get out of my ear!" Rodney shouted, hitting the other side of his head with his palm as if the force of physics would knock that fly out. "That doesn't make any sense! Why should I hit myself in the head? Like when a swimmer has water in her ears after swimming, she'll jump up and down with her head tilted as if the water would just drain out of her ear. But what about her other ear? Wouldn't the water just drill right into her brains? Why do people do that to themselves? So what should I do about this fly? Maybe I should just stand here and wait till he decides to fly out. Try not to think about it. Hmmm. I don't think that's gonna be so easy. After all, I got a fly in my ear. He's got no choice, right? He's gotta fly away at some time. I don't s'pose he could feast on earwax. I don't s'pose he could actually enter my brain like water?"

Just then the fly entered Rodney's brain. The little insect maneuvered itself to a place in the corner of Rodney's mind where it could see out of Rodney's shining eye.

"How boring this view is," the fly remarked, "these humans are nearly blind -- their vision is so limited. Nonetheless, I like the sparkly thing in this one."

"What do you mean by that?" Rodney thought back.

"I mean, you humans have these huge clumsy simple eyes. I always thought that you guys could see so much out of them. Hmmm. No wonder you could never catch one of us," the fly responded.

"That's right. You flies got those complex eyes!" Rodney remembered from Biology. "How do you make sense of all the fragments you must see at the same time? I wonder if it's anything like seeing all of time all at once."

The fly contemplated that thought, "Well, I don't think it's like that, because we don't see everything in its entirety. We just see bits of everything. Like sampling."

"What's sampling?"

"Sampling is having a little of everything. Like if me and a friend were to invade some human's picnic. Maybe my friend likes the Sloppy Joes, so he spends the afternoon buzzing around that dish. But me, I try a little of everything -- some corn, some chili, some jelly, some pie ... "

"Some dog poop!"

"Hey don't knock it till you try it. Anyway, I think you're getting the idea of sampling. Can't you see that I'd have a more informed opinion about human food than my friend?"

"Yea, I s'pose that'd be true."

"That's sampling. We Earthlings don't have time to understand everything entirely, but we can sample. It's the big picture. It makes your sight richer. You humans see like TV, just one square view, you can't see what's above, below or to the sides of that square."

"Wow, pretty interesting insight for a bug."

"Thank you -- I have to learn quick you know. My life is only a couple of weeks long."

Rodney ruminated over this latest insight, "Hey, but if you guys can see so well, why do you have so many problems with windows."

"Glass! I hate glass! You got me there. I fall for it every time. Ram my little head right into it."

"I s'pose we humans have been known to run into a glass door every once in a while."

"None of us are perfect -- but when it comes to complex eyes, us flies got 'em. That's how we can buzz around in fast random paths without getting dizzy."

"I'd love to know what it'd be like to see out of your eyes."

"I'm impressed with your open-mindedness, kid. Most humans aren't even interested in trying to understand the viewpoints of other humans -- let alone a seemingly insignificant insect such as a fly."

"Yea but, I don't s'pose I'd fit inside your mind. Besides I'm already in my author's."

"Is your author a fly?"

"Oh, that would have worked! But I've already checked -- he's human."

"Perhaps you could ask your author to imagine a very big fly so that you could crawl inside its mind and be able to see through its eyes."

"Crazed! I'll try it!" Rodney stood up straight and cleared his throat as if he were Dorothy addressing the Great Wizard of Oz, "Ahhmmm, excuse me my author, but if it wouldn't take you too much from your storyline, could you please imagine a large fly so that I could crawl inside its mind?"

There was a long pause, as if Rodney's author was thinking about that proposal off in some distant part of his brain. (Which, in fact, he was.) The author chuckled to himself, wondering if he should answer Rodney directly or just go ahead and imagine a mammoth fly. He decided to just go ahead and imagine a mammoth fly.

Rodney stumbled a few steps back, the buzzing was deafening and the little fly inside Rodney's mind thought, "Man! Is that what we sound like??!! That's really annoying!"

The mammoth fly landed in front of Rodney. Its body could easily hide a football field. The wind from its wings knocked Rodney to the ground. Its complex eyes, each the size of Rodney's house, hovered intimidatingly near.

"Looks like your author has been accommodating," the little fly in Rodney's brain commented, "pretty ugly, huh? That's what you guys look like to us!"

"Well ... I asked for it -- didn't I?" Rodney remarked as he studied the beast for a crevice to crawl into. Finding one on the side of its head -- he climbed inside, "Crazed! I'm in the brain of a fly with a fly in my brain all inside the brain of my author."

"How cozy," mused the little fly in Rodney's brain.

Rodney muttered to himself, "It's like Benj's ivory concentric balls."

"Just down the next bend you'll find a nice place to look outside of its eyes," directed the little fly in Rodney's brain.

Rodney turned the corner and a kaleidoscope of light, colors, and images exploded into him, "This is what it feel's like when Warm Face taps me on the shoulder."

The mammoth fly took off into the air and the kaleidoscope rotated thirty degrees and then one hundred and seventy and then another forty-five the other direction. Rodney fell to his knees in nausea and threw up for several minutes. The sky turned into night and then into a sheet of glass, which could not be seen through the complex eyes of the mammoth fly. The mammoth fly jerked into the glass, shattering it into minute specks of grain that twinkled like stars and Rodney imagined himself a shooting star falling through fields of black space into a garden of solid Earth.

The bull disappeared in a small valley and reappeared only a moment or two later, ten feet away from Dan. It stopped, held its head up strong and peered deeply into Dan's eyes. Dan hadn't taken another breath since he held it moments before ... finally he gasped sharply. The bull shuttered, the hair on its back raised, its horns lowered, and it charged ten feet straight into the shaking Dan. Dan flipped in the air twice and landed flat on his back, "There! Now it happened! I always knew it would! Geeze, all those years in the elevator, I step out for five minutes and I get rammed off my feet! Rodney! Get me out of this part of the story!"

"Dan, Dan, calm down. You're not even scratched. Think of it. The thing you been hiding from all your life has just happened. And you're still alive. Don't ya feel freed?" Rodney helped Dan to his feet, "Look at that bull, licking up the apple seeds you dropped. He likes them," Rodney reached into his pockets and pulled out another handful, "here's some more. Try again, Dan."

Dan stood back up. The fear had been knocked out of him and he walked straight to the bull with his open hand, "I will make friends with the bull. I will make friends with the bull."

The bull finished the last seed on the ground and looked up at Dan and nothing happened.

"Ah, Dan. I think it's the armor," Warm Face suggested, "I think he doesn't like you wearing that armor -- he thinks you're trying to intimidate him."

"Oh! Great! I knew it would come to this," Dan whined to himself. "Okay, I'm tired of fearing you. Here I am. Kill me or be my friend," Dan gently removed his protective shields until only his street clothes remained.

The bull raised its head peacefully up to Dan's, looked him in the eye for just a second more and began to lick the seeds from his hand.

"Did you see that look he gave me?" Dan beamed as he pet the bull like a puppy. "It was as if he was proud of me! As if he respected me!"

"I saw it," Warm Face confirmed, "I saw it in your eyes too."

Dan laughed, "Look at me, I'm feeding this bull!"

"Dan, I believed in you. I really did," Shining Eye continued, "And now that you have won the bull over as your new friend, I'd appreciate it greatly if you request that he tip this large rock so that I can plant a seed underneath it."

"Shining Eye! What a splendid plan!" Warm Face exclaimed. "The seed will grow into a tree and carry the star up above the ground, so that in sixty years when the wind slings come it will be twenty-five feet high and they'll be able to slingshot it back into space. It's a wonderful contribution, Shining Eye, I am very proud of you right now."

"Okay, Okay, I'm impressed with this get-to-know-the-bull trick. But even if I could persuade the bull to tip your rock -- there's no light under there and the weight of the rock alone would prevent the seed from making any progress," Dan whined pessimistically, "Do you really expect this apple seed to grow where nothing at all can grow?"

"Yes, I do," Rodney whined optimistically, "besides

it's not really a matter of can or cannot. Look, if some guy plants twenty seeds and only one grows, should he feel bad because nearly all of them did not?"

Dan made a strange face and scratched his head with his left hand.

"Of course not -- he made a whole tree!" Rodney exclaimed as if it were cracked-open obvious, "Who cares if a hundred seeds never quite made it?"

"I know a woman who makes a file," Warm Face expanded, "she documents each of her failures and is proud of every one. She says it means she's out there trying."

Dan lowered his head a bit and kicked himself in the butt, "She's probably not in some elevator wearing armor afraid of life or something."

"And a whole tree where there was nothing before ... that changes the universe forever," Warm Face continued. "Birds will nest in it, families will picnic in its shade, lovers will carve their names and kiss under it, maybe monkeys will play in it, cats will dodge dogs up it. And just think of all the apples! Apples have seeds you know, perhaps in two hundred years a new orchard will emerge here."

Rodney paused to take a breath, "I mean, yea, you're right, I can think of better places to plant seeds, but if this one grows ... if this single seed grows, Daniel, we'll have sent a shooting star back into space! Think of it! I've only got seventy more years of life left, tops. I want to make a positive difference. I think that even if this seed doesn't quite make it, the small amount of time it will take to plant it -- will be time well spent. Already, look at you. Standing there with your head high, petting a bull you feared for almost two decades. You got out of the elevator in spite of the odds. Why not give this seed the same chance? Isn't it all the same thing?"

Warm Face watched Rodney's shining eye in great admiration as he spoke, and she added as he finished, "We can't be sure that this seed will grow; but we can be certain that a tree will not grow without a seed."

"It's such a small thing, Dan." Rodney summed, "but its potential's real great. The odds aren't good -- but even one hundred to one still makes it possible."

"Okay, plant your seed -- I was just saying ... " Dan said defensively. "I wasn't telling you not to. I was just expressing my opinion about the practicality here," Dan mumbled as he nearly instinctually led the bull over to the rock. The bull licked up the last few seeds, leaned its head forward and tipped the rock as far as it could.

CHAPTER 12

Rodney smiled and reached into his pocket for just one seed. He crawled up to the rock and reached with his hand under it, "There's not enough space. I can't reach to the center. I need a longer arm."

"Or a small burrowing animal," Warm Face suggested.

Rodney, lying belly on the ground, reaching like a mechanic under a car, turned to Warm Face in frustration, "Thanks, do you happen to have a hamster on you?"

"A hamster?" asked the racecar driver, "Look, don't you worry about that one. I got lots of extras."

"Extra whats?" Rodney tried to look back and see who was talking.

"Lugs!" the racecar driver answered, "Do you think I'd let us lose time over a stupid lug nut? Now come on outta there -- I already got the spare on."

Rodney pulled himself out of the crevice in the side of a huge cliff and brushed himself off, "Where are we?"

"You're the bloke with the map -- you tell me!" the driver snipped as he got back in the fire red sports car.

Rodney climbed into the passenger seat and picked up a map of Western Europe. He ran his finger along the path marked in red ink all the way up to, "BELGIUM!"

"Brilliant Chap. Now would you please put on your belt and helmet so we can get back on track?"

"Helmet?"

"Yes! Your helmet! So your head won't splatter all over the windshield if I nod off or somethin'," the British driver squinted his eyes in a somewhat disturbed fashion, "what's gotten' into you ol' boy?"

"A helmet sounds like a real good idea."

"Yes, of course! I love speed. But, I'm no dimwit. This stuff can kill you. It ain't that hard to take a few precautions -- and it don't take none o' the thrill away, neither. My heart still gets ta sputterin' on the open road. You know?"

"I know, but only in fantasy. Reality's bit more difficult."

" ... And a heck of a lot more dangerous as well!"

"Yea, that too."

"Ah, but it's worth it, boy, ain't it? The taste of the wind, the blur of the trees, the resonatin' treads rocking the car back an' forth. Ain't it worth it though?"

"I told Dan to take his armor off. Am I a dimwit?"

"Come again, chap?"

"Dan was in an elevator for twenty years. He wore a full suit of Armor from head to toe because he was afraid of his own life."

"I don't know Dan's story, maybe it'd help for me to tell you that I don't be sleepin' with my helmet on. And you won't find me carrying' salt in the trunk in the summer, neither. That would only slow me down. I'm willin' to take the risk of bein' caught in an August snow without it. Follow me, chum?"

"Kinda. It's like keepin' seedlings in an inside pot so that they won't be eaten by insects or frozen by the cold. But then their growth gets cut. They never get to be what they're s'posed to be."

"Somethin' like that. Life is dangerous. It ain't so bad to get scraped and bruised by it -- that's much better than missin' the good parts -- like speed. But when something can kill you or permanently mess you up, you gotta take some measures of protection. You gotta shield yourself enough to cut down the probability of permanent damage -- but not so much so that the fun gets cut out."

"And the helmet isn't that heavy."

"Right! It's a bit freer to be without it, but it still ain't that bad, and you get real used to it. And speed ... it's still speed with or without the helmet. I'm still just as fast." The driver paused in thought, "Patrick, one of my best friends ever -- he was killed bein' too macho to wear it ... or too stupid. Speed can change your life forever. An accident can happen any time. Gotta wear it every time you're racing. Every time."

"I encouraged Dan to face the bull without his armor."

"Hmmm. I don't know the situation, chap. I just know speed. It takes Petrol for speed. Ain't no way around that. And petrol can blow you into a hundred pieces."

"I know how that feels."

"It's your call, boy. It's Dan's call. Each of us has to look at the possible exhilarations and the possible destructions that are spin-offs of every risk -- or in not taking any risk, for that matter. How much protection is up to each of us. And then without ignorin' the dangers -- make our choices. But to be honest, the elevator plan sounded like a downer to me."

"I see. So, the only one who knows if it was a good call is Dan?"

"You can only do so much. Sometimes you can be completely prepared and still get hit by a falling rock. Speed's funny like that. You only go around once. May as well enjoy the race."

"So what do you think? Was it a good call or not?"

"Well it seems to me that this bloke Dan, wasn't really livin' much anyway. I mean, yea, a bull could have possibly killed him. But sometimes it takes a high risk to resuscitate a dead guy -- a good whack in the butt. The real test is time. Let's see if he doesn't put his armor back on." The driver smiled, "Hey, but enough of this heady stuff -- be a chum, reach under that seat and get me a candy bar."

Rodney bent, feeling with his outstretched fingers under the seat, he grabbed the furry animal, "A hamster! I could use one of these!"

"Aye! He's me good luck charm," the Irish driver explained.

"Geeze, You scared me half to death," Rodney gasped in the realization that he was now in a different car with a different driver, probably in a different race all together.

"And ya, me, laddie. How'd ya git in heere? I dreve alone. Were ya hidin' unda da seat then?" the driver asked, more intrigued than frightened.

"I'm not sure myself sir. But if you don't mind, I'd really like to borrow this hamster for another part of the story. It would only take a second."

"Sure son, don't ya be worryin' yaself none. We'd be glad ta oblige."

Rodney sighed and put the hamster up on the dashboard to look him in the face and play with his whiskers.

"So what ya t'ink o' I'lan', boy?" the driver asked.

"Ireland?" Rodney looked out the window into Ireland, "Wow, sure is pretty."

"'Me 'omeland -- I'lan' be."

The road wound like Christmas tree garland around the green mountains. The engine called out softly to the wind, which blew through Rodney's hair. And then came the bull.

The driver swerved sharply to the left to avoid it, which caused the hamster to slide the distance of the dashboard to Rodney's window. Rodney lunged forward and nabbed the hamster by its hind legs just as it became airborne.

"That was a close one!" Rodney shouted, "We almost lost your good luck charm!"

"Aye! But dat sure be a t'rill, aye laddie?" the driver said, "so laddie, what people be callin' ya?"

"Rodney sir."

"Rodney sir? Hmm. Well dat dere be Henry and I dey be callin' Patty -- Rodney sir." the driver chuckled.

"Patty as in Patrick?"

"Aye."

Rodney looked down and noticed that they were not wearing seat belts. He quickly fastened his own and cautioned Patty to do the same.

"Lad, I'm fast, but I be good at dis wheel. Seat belts -- dey be for women an' boys."

And that's when the passing truck blew a tire and slid into Patty's sports car. Rodney ducked under the dashboard.

"Looks like the boy is stuck in pretty snug," the first paramedic said.

The second paramedic took his hand from Patrick's wrist and shook his head, "We lost this one."

"Well the boy's still breathing," the first paramedic

maneuvered himself so that he could shine his penlight into Rodney's simple eyeballs, "His pupils are normal, probably he's dreamin'. Hey, his left eye has silver in it. Like silver in stone. It's eerie."

"We're not here to fall in love, Bobby," said the second, "Now get the grease and let's slide the kid outta there."

The paramedics greased Rodney up and slid him out of the crinkled car like a watermelon seed.

Rodney came to a couple of moments later, "What happened?"

"You were involved in an automobile accident," the first paramedic informed Rodney, "you've got a couple of nice bumps on your head, but you'll be okay."

Rodney looked at Patty and started to cry, "I was just making the connection. I was just gonna try to make him wear his seat belt. I knew this would happen! I was just with his friend who told me it would."

"Take it easy son. There was nothin' you could've done," the first paramedic consoled.

The second paramedic notice something moving in the car, "Hey did you folks have a pet in here?"

"Henry!" Wiping his tears away with the back of his forearms, Rodney reached somberly through the window and under the seat.

CHAPTER 13

"What are you looking for?" Rodney's mom asked.

"Mom!"

"Yes, Rodney?"

"Mom, I love you."

"I love you too Rodney," Rodney's mom replied, "but it really worries me when you stray off like that. When we get home I want you to promise your father and I that you'll be more careful about our feelings."

Rodney smiled to be back in the Volvo with his mom. He looked down to make sure they both were wearing their belts -- they were. "There isn't a hamster in the car -- is there?" before his mom could answer he rolled down his window and pulled down on his cheeks so that he could get a good look at his eyes, "There's nothing in my eyes!" he exclaimed.

"Good. Was something bothering you?"

Rodney grabbed at his messy hair, "And my head

isn't bumped and my hair ain't greasy!"

Rodney's mom looked over at her son, "Rodney, what have you been doin' today?"

Rodney sighed a big sigh, "I've been learnin' a lot."

"That's good. My mother used to tell me to never stop learning. Never."

The Volvo pulled up to the home of the Appleseeds and Rodney hopped out fast. He ran up to Randy's house inspecting the area for bullet holes. There were none.

The Appleseeds had a very normal dinner complete with the TV blaring. Afterwards, Rodney gave Chance a big hug and she kicked him in the kneecap.

"What did you do that for?" She moaned.

"Because you're my sister and I just want you to know that I care about you," Rodney answered. "Why did you kick me?"

"Because you're my brother and we're just kids." Chance's grimace turned into a grin, she looked Rodney warmly in the eyes and ran away.

Rodney smiled too, then walked over to his father who was looking for a new location for the television.

"How about over here? Rodney, what do you think?"

"That's great dad. Do you love me?"

"That's great dad. Do I love you? What have you been doin' today, Rodney?"

"I've been thinkin' a lot."

"Great. Well, yes, of course I love you. Now grab

this cord and plug it in under the table for me."

Rodney took hold of the cord, started to reach under the table with it and then paused.

"What's up son, can't you reach?"

"No that's not it dad. I can reach."

"So ... then why are you not reaching?"

Rodney slowly, calmly, let a breath of air out and plugged the end of the cord into the wall. He closed his eyes and pulled himself out from under the table to see his dad adjusting the antenna. Rodney sighed.

"Thanks son."

"My pleasure pop. Hey, 'mind if I use the phone?"

"Go right ahead."

Rodney hopped over to the family phone, looked around the corner towards his dad, picked up the receiver and listened to the dial tone for just a moment, "Hello God?" he whispered only half jokingly.

Rodney's father leaned back and turned his head in Rodney's direction, "Who are you calling, son?!!"

"Randy, dad," Rodney quickly replied.

Rodney's father leaned forward shaking his head, he mumbled under his breath, "I don't like that Randy kid."

'976-233 ...' Rodney paused, checked the windows, put one hand on the top of his head, ducked, and then dialed the last digit ... '4', "Hello, may I please talk with Randy?"

"Rodman! What's happening bud?" Randy answered.

"How's your knee?"

"My knee? How's your knees?"

"My knee? You're the one ... " Rodney stopped himself, "Ah, forget it."

"Rod, you're a loon man. But hey, you got any cans? Let's pop cans tonight!!!"

"I might be a loon, but you're crazed!"

"Okay, I can live with that. Get some cans and meet me in the alley behind the prairie. Over?"

"Over and out, Randman."

Rodney hung up and headed for the kitchen. He stood in front of the trash bag for a moment and then reached in through the mashed potatoes, corn bits, and fatty scraps from dinner, to the lone slimy corn can. Holding it up with just his thumb and pointing finger, he rinsed it off in the sink. After that unpleasantry was done, he grabbed his shoes. "I'll be out in the alley with Randy, be home in an hour!" Rodney forewarned, remembering what his mother had said.

The flimsy back door whacked shut as Rodney's mother and father stepped into the back kitchen. The kitchen faucet dripped in the clumsy silence.

"I don't like Rodney playing with that Randy kid," Rodney's father stated firmly.

"Calm down Frank -- they're just kids," Rodney's mother replied.

Frank Appleseed shook his head again and walked back to the TV, "That Randy kid is gonna be in jail before he's twenty."

Rodney had been on the back steps tying his shoes.

He heard his father's words through the door. Randy was Rodney's best friend; it hurt to learn that his father didn't trust him. On the other hand, the jail bit didn't seem too far-fetched.

With that familiar thoughtful look on his face, Rodney walked over to the shed, pulled the unlatched padlock from the door and looked inside. He grabbed a bag and put the corn can in it along with some other things from the shed.

Randy was sitting by the Bensons' fence in the dark waiting as Rodney hobbled up to him.

"Man. Do you have any idea how hard it is to sit here with half a brick of firecrackers and not light any of them?!!!" Randy popped.

"Geeze, it was only five minutes!"

"So ... ???!!"

"Besides, you could have blown off a couple without me."

"Rodster, you're my bud. I wouldn't have liked it if you popped off a couple without me."

"Okay Randy, you're right. I'm sorry. Here, I could only find one can."

Randy kicked a turkey tin full of cans out from the dark, "Rodman, I know you too well."

Rodney shrugged and grinned at the healthy arsenal.

Randy stood up, peeking in Rodney's sack, "What else you got in the bag?"

Rodney pulled the bottom of the bag up and dumped its contents: a box of long stick matches, two pairs of his father's heavy work gloves and a couple of swimming masks, "It won't be that hard to use this stuff -- and the cans will fly just as high."

"Swimming masks?"

Rodney grabbed one and strapped it on, "See, no problem, and it really cuts down the chances of permanent damage."

" ... a loon, bud, a real loon," Randy muttered as he strapped on the other mask and slipped his hands into a pair of the oversize gloves, "T-10 seconds!"

Mr. Johnson watched from his window on the third floor of the old 4810 house. A single peachish alley light silhouetted the two boys in the night. Every forty seconds or so their faces would glow with the orange spark of the firecrackers as well as the warmth of their own excitement. The soaring cans could be seen from Jerson's Candy Stop Shop two blocks over. The boys' laughter could be heard even inside the Appleseed's home. Chance ran to the window and watched.

Randy smiled wildly and pulled a blasting cap from his pocket, "My dad used to use these, back when he was loggin' in the Kentucky backwoods. It should send your corn can into orbit, bud!"

Rodney shrugged his shoulders and stepped back without a word. Randy, surprised at the absence of some kind of pragmatic warning, struck a long stick match on the sidewalk and very carefully lit the wick -- the very short wick.

The crack was bright and momentarily blinding, like

a camera's flash. Smoke and soot blasted out from under the can in all directions. There was a bit of an air burst too, but it was mostly the surprise that knocked Randy backwards on his butt. The soot covered the two boys. By the time they wiped it from their swimming goggles, the can was practically out of sight.

"Whoa! Did you see that?!?!" Randy shouted.

Rodney just watched in silence until the corn can was clearly out of view. They both waited for it to land or at least see it come back down. They waited almost a whole minute.

"Crazed! Maybe it did make it into orbit!" Randy exclaimed in excitement.

"Maybe even all the way to infinity ... " Rodney calmly and peacefully replied.

"That's it. That's the last can. The others are off in the prairie and it's way too dark to find them now."

"So it was a good night. Let's call it quits, Randman."

"Hold on bud, I still have about ten crackers left and this turkey tin ... get the picture ... ???" Randy hinted.

Again, Rodney offered no words of caution, he figured that they were pretty well protected with the long matches, masks and gloves. Randy strung the eleven long-wicked firecrackers together and tucked them strategically under the tin. He turned to Rodney and handed him the last long match, "Rodman, would you like to do the honors?"

Rodney grinned, knelt on one knee, struck the

match and turned his head back towards Randy, "You know, my good friend, this is what it's like when I'm off thinking ... all those sparkling cans gliding through space, they're my thoughts. This night is what it's like when I think."

"You know Rodney, you think too much." The small flame reflected off his mask as Randy shook his head and broke into a smirk, "Sometimes you just gotta have fun."

Rodney kept his eyes fixed on Randy's carbon covered face. Looking deep into Randy's eyes he spoke with great care, "And sometimes you just gotta think."

Randy put his lower lip up under his teeth and nodded ever so subtly. Rodney faced the tin, as he reached under it with the match he whispered, "Maybe, me and you, maybe we can learn a lot from each other."

CHAPTER 14

"Haven't we been doing that all along, Shining Eye?" Warm Face asked in return. "Look, you want to plant that seed directly in the center under the rock -- don't you? You are a powerful person, but you can't do it. You were smart enough to get the bull to move the rock, why must you insist on planting the seed yourself? Use your resources. And I didn't exactly have a hamster in mind."

"Geeze!" Rodney remembered, "and I had a hamster in my hands not too long ago." He paused in recollection, "Yea, but you're right. It's just that, I really love planting seeds you know."

Warm Face nodded, "I know."

"Well," Rodney backed out from under the rock, the carbon still covering the lower half of his face, "What other burrowing animals might be around here?"

Warm Face paused a bit to give Rodney a chance to

think it out for himself, but oddly enough he was not thinking well, "Uhmm, I'm not sure that it is exactly classified as a burrowing animal -- but how about a squirrel?" She finally offered.

"Good idea! Only I don't see any around right now," Rodney commented, a bit disheartened over his inability to plant the seed himself, as well as a bit concerned about his previous encouragement to Dan to shed his armor.

Warm Face pointed West, "There's a group of trees only a couple of minutes that way. Why don't you go have a look?"

"Okay, thanks. I'll do that," Shining Eye stood to his feet. Slowly regaining some of his usual optimism, he brushed the dirt from his torn jeans, shook his messy hair, nodded at Warm Face and Dan, and then scampered off to the small forest.

Dan let the bull relax and shook his head, "This is crazy."

"Yea," Warm Face countered, "but, you were born without your own permission and your heart pumps blood through your body, and all your organs are working to keep you functioning and you don't even know how or why -- that's really crazy."

Dan made that same strange face and scratched his head again.

Dusk took over the clouded sky, thin shavings of the melon sun folded over the landscape as Rodney approached the silent forest. Even the birds were quiet.

"Hey squirrel!" Rodney shouted, feeling a bit silly. "We need a squirrel!"

The forest swayed gently in the soft cool breeze, but offered up not a single burrowing animal.

"This forest is empty!" Rodney thought to himself. He stepped up to it and grabbed a tree. The tree felt good in his hands and he shook it until hang-gliding leaves sported in and out around the trunk and Rodney. But no squirrels.

A bit dispirited, Rodney lifted his feet and dashed with his arms out like an airplane directly to the center of the forest, "Squirrels! Squirrels! Are there any squirrels?"

A monkey reached from his home in a tree and fwacked Rodney in the face as he ran by. The slap knocked Rodney on his butt. "You're no squirrel!" Rodney shouted up at the monkey.

The monkey jumped from the tree and waddled peacefully to Rodney sitting in the leaves. Face to face, the monkey peered right into Rodney's eyes, "Think, small man! Think, higher primate. You humans fancy yourselves so much smarter than us, but look at you ... you can't even find a squirrel in a forest!" is what the monkey might have said if it could talk. But it couldn't, so it slapped Shining Eye square in the face a second time.

"I get it!" Rodney jumped to his feet, "Thank you, you little ape. I owe you one."

The monkey nodded and waddled off. Rodney

reached into his pocket and pulled out an apple seed, which ignited an ominous reverberating ticking clatter. It was the sound of three dozen or so hiding squirrels, each on a tree of its own, each clawing its way around the trunk into full view of Rodney's shining eye. Rodney stood in awe of the magnificent sound. His mouth gaped widely in the welcome presence of the furry creatures that he had only moments before thought completely absent. Grinning, he held his single apple seed up to the sky. The squirrels paused in a statue silence for a moment, until finally, a young squirrel darted down its tree, across the brush and straight up Rodney. The tiny nails pinched Rodney's arm as the squirrel perched on its hind legs, and cupping its front paws around Rodney's hand, nibbled at the seed. After it finished, the squirrel ran back down Rodney's arm and sat attentively on his shoulder. Rodney, beaming ear to ear, started back to the garden, the squirrel on his shoulder bounced easily along, while all the other squirrels scurried back invisibly around their respective trunks to nonexistence.

Dan could see Rodney approaching, so with a pat on the back of his bull, the large rock was once again tipped.

Warm Face called out, "Good job, Shining Eye! Who's your new friend?"

"Well ... How about Rocky?" Shining Eye recommended in tribute.

"Does he fly?" Dan joked.

"I don't know. Let's see ... " Rodney bent his shoulder toward Dan. Rocky leaped six feet through the air to Dan's head.

Dan turned his slightly crossed eyes upward, "Hey, great hang time! Sign him up!"

Warm Face giggled, "He really is a flying squirrel!"

"Okay, Okay, Rocky, and now for something we'll really like," Rodney jested as he reached into his pocket for the last of his daily supply of apple seeds.

Rocky dove from Dan's head to the ground, swiping the seed from Rodney's hand on the way! Without hesitation, Rocky swallowed the seed whole.

Shocked, the three stood dumbfounded. Rodney closed his eyes tightly in frustration and put his head down into his hands. Mrs. Finkelstein put her arm around him and walked down the soft quiet hallway, "Come now Rodney, it's only a squirrel, it doesn't hate you. It's only playing. You can't take these things so seriously. You said that yourself. You can have my recess, Rodney, but I will not allow you to worry yourself like this. You made good choices. You trusted yourself at every turn. You were careful and yet you never gave up the search for truth. You worked with good in mind. And you had fun. Didn't you have fun? You can't tell me now that you didn't."

Rodney moped alongside, comfortable in the warm hug of Mrs. Finkelstein.

"Come on," Mrs. Finkelstein encouraged, "I want you to see something. It's my small positive contribution to you."

The elderly teacher led the quiet boy into an empty classroom. She squinted at the bookcase for several minutes and then pulled out a physics book. "Let's see: Measures, Medians, Modes, Moebius, Ah ... Molecules - freezing of."

Mrs. Finkelstein opened the book and began explaining why ice floats in a manner that Rodney could understand. The big hand on the old clock above the blackboard nearly completed its circle before Rodney looked up and scratched his head like Dan. Then, in that moment of enlightenment, realizing how thick he'd been, he slapped his hands over his face.

"And one other thing," Mrs. Finkelstein informed hesitantly, "red doesn't mean anything to bulls. They're colorblind. It's the movement that get's 'em riled up."

"Really?"

"Really."

Rodney slapped his forehead one more time.

Rocky made a snickering sound, spat the seed back into his front paw, scurried to the center underneath the tilted boulder, buried the moistened apple seed, and scampered off contentedly to the forest, pleased with his contribution.

The bull gently rolled the rock back to resting position and the three leaned against it with a simultaneous sigh. Dan started to speak, but was interrupted by a very short fellow that appeared out of nowhere sitting cross-legged on the rock.

The short fellow spoke, "So what's it gonna be?"

"What's what gonna be?" Rodney retorted.

"Your wish -- what's it gonna be? Gold? All the money in the universe? A cute blonde?" the short fellow grinned as he pulled a pencil and a small notebook from his pocket.

"A wish ... I get a wish!" Rodney realized out loud.

"Yea, sure, well one of you here does," the fellow continued, "after all, you were right, this is a genuine shooting star. And leaning as you are, it is your right to wish upon it."

Dan pointed out, "I'm leaning upon it too ... "

"Yes and so is the young lady," the fellow went on, "but, I'm sorry, there's only one wish per star per planet. I'm already making a special exception by coming here in person. I usually just jot down the wishes as they come in. But you all look like nice folks and I was really touched with what you're trying to do here. Such a noble contribution -- returning a shooting star to the universe. Actually, it's very rare that we lose a cruiser like this, you know."

Rodney nodded, "Thanks for coming by in person."

"Will it increase our chances of getting our wish granted?" Dan nudged.

"Not really," the wish-giver explained. "Each wish is documented and submitted. But there are no guarantees -- except that some do get granted. No one knows which or why. So comrades, what's it gonna be?"

Warm Face spoke, "I think that since the whole idea was Rodney's, that he should be the one to make the wish."

Dan nodded in agreement.

Rodney looked down to the ground in thought and began cleaning his ear with his finger, "Would you be able to give me all the answers to every question in the universe?"

"Sure, piece of cake," the fellow assured.

"The reason for our existence, the point of life, why golfers shout 'FOUR' and all of that?" Rodney expanded.

"No, problem. All topics covered -- from innocence to war to every question you'll ever be asked on every exam for the rest of your life," the short fellow offered. "Is that what you'd like then?"

"Hmmmmm ... " Rodney twisted his finger for several more minutes. Warm Face squinted her eyes patiently, ready to assist if Rodney started to become the ball again. Dan thought of the thing he'd always wished for -- being out in the world unafraid.

"No." Rodney lifted his head, "Just get me a horse for my sister."

The short fellow scratched a note down and faded away into the post-dusk sky. Warm Face smiled in grand approval, kissed Shining Eye warmly on the forehead and, putting her arm around Dan, escorted him and the bull gently out of Rodney's dream. Rodney just stood there in a peaceful stupor, smiling.

The breeze became stronger and quite cool, pulling the night clouds from the sky, opening it to Rodney like stage curtains.

Walking with Warm Face, Dan asked, "Do you think the seed will really grow? And even if it does, do you think that the wind slings will really come sixty years from now?"

"I don't think. I dream," Warm Face answered warmly.

"I'm really not into this philosophical stuff," Dan responded, "My brain hurts. I don't want to think anymore. All that I know is that I am much happier today than I have been in twenty years. I feel great!"

"Me too, Dan," Warm Face responded with a dreamy smile, "me too."

When every cloud had drifted away, the tiny suns began to twinkle and create an illusion of glass. Rodney stepped carefully between the roses and tulips to a field of tall grass, dandelions and corn. He ran with his hands in the air, picked up a stone and threw it into the sky of glass. The stone sailed so high that Rodney could no longer see it, until a crashing thunderbolt broke hard against the mountains and the night shattered into infinitely many crystal chips. The chips melted as they entered Earth's atmosphere into drops of water. Some fell on Rodney (making streaks in the carbon on his chin), some fell in Rodney's kitchen sink, and still others fell on the apple seed planted by the old woman who was not Rodney's mom.

And the woman who was not Rodney's mom went out to the front yard to gently stroke the seedling. Drizzle fell to the ground along with a single stone. The woman picked up the stone, which had fallen on the third square. She put it in her pocket and hopped: 1, 2, 4&5, 6, 7&8, 9, Sky Blue!

... And The Credits Rolled ...

twinkle
twinkle
little star
how i wonder
where you are
up above
the earth
so high
like a
diamond
in the sky
twinkle
twinkle
little star
how i wonder

Did you enjoy Rodney Appleseed?

1) Tell everyone you know
2) Then tell Ross:

Ross@RossAnthony.com
(Subject: Appleseed!)

3) One last thing

Check out other Ross Anthony books at

www.RossAnthony.com/books

(And read his free essays & articles while you're there.)

Books sometimes become movies and movies get reviewed at...

www.RossAnthony.com

Film Reviews and Interviews

ORDER FORM

Credit Card orders: accepted online 24/7 with fast delivery @
www.RossAnthony.com/Books

Check / Money orders: First check all prices at
www.RossAnthony.com/books. Then use this form and send a
check payable to Ross Anthony by post (little snail mail) to:

Ross Anthony / AZB
P.O. Box 5
Pasadena, CA 91102

⬛ " **RODNEY APPLESEED** in Nothing Happens" $9.95*
"It is the best book I have ever read!" Julie, RN.
Quantity x Price* = Rodney Subtotal
_____ x _____ + = _____

⬛ **"THE LITTLE SNAIL STORY"** $8.95*
"Incredible -- Four Stars!" www.SmartGirl.org review.
Quantity x Price* = Snail Subtotal
_____ x _____ + = _____

⬛ **FREE** new book alert newsletter $0.00

Rodney Subtotal + Snail Subtotal + S/H* + CA Tax* = **TOTAL**
_____ + _____ + ___ + _____ = _____

YOUR NAME:_____

ADDRESS:_____

City_____State_____Zip_____
                    Email _____

US RESIDENTS: **Shipping/Handling: $3.50***
*These Prices valid 2003 only: reference RossAnthony.com/books.
CALIFORNIA RESIDENTS: Please add 8.25%* sales tax.
INTERNATIONAL ORDERING: books@rossanthony.com (Subject: APPLESEED).
(Photocopy permission is granted for this page only.)

INTERNATIONAL ORDERING: books@rossanthony.com (Subject: APPLESEED).
(Photocopy permission is granted for this page only.)

Also by Ross Anthony

Books

The Little Snail Story

Like Saint-Exupery's "Little Prince," disguised as a children's
book, "Little Snail" is a timeless story of gathering understanding,
trust and belief in oneself. Can Snail find the courage to leave the
comfort and security of Shell? A friendly, insightful encouraging
story for anyone hesitant to live an enriching vivacious life.
**For more on this and other Ross Anthony books:
www.RossAnthony.com/books.**

Short Essays

Zen of Surfing
A River Runs Through You
Graduation Boy
In the Dark (A 911 Tribute)

Read these essays for free at RossAnthony.com/books.

Celebrity Interviews

Harrison Ford
Meg Ryan
Michelle Pfeiffer
Johnny Knoxville
Antonio Banderas, etc.